(some of) verla volante's Ideas About Writing

A good writer tells the truth by telling lies.

When you're talking to a character, you find out what they think and feel. But what a character feels isn't always true.

Pay attention. Notice things and think about what you notice.

Sometimes you're writing about one thing and you realize that you're really writing about something else.

You can work on a story while you're doing anything that doesn't engage your whole attention.

Anything that doesn't kill you makes you stronger. And later on you can use it in some story.

Other Books You May Enjoy

the Wild Girls

PAT MURPHY

speak

An Imprint of Penguin Group (USA) Inc.

SPEAK
Published by the Penguin Group
Penguin Group (USA) Inc., 345 Hudson Street, New York, New York 10014, U.S.A.
Penguin Group (Canada), 90 Eglinton Avenue East, Suite 700, Toronto, Ontario, Canada M4P 2Y3
(a division of Pearson Penguin Canada Inc.)
Penguin Books Ltd, 80 Strand, London WC2R 0RL, England
Penguin Ireland, 25 St Stephen's Green, Dublin 2, Ireland (a division of Penguin Books Ltd)
Penguin Group (Australia), 250 Camberwell Road, Camberwell, Victoria 3124, Australia
(a division of Pearson Australia Group Pty Ltd)
Penguin Books India Pvt Ltd, 11 Community Centre, Panchsheel Park, New Delhi - 110 017, India
Penguin Group (NZ), 67 Apollo Drive, Rosedale, North Shore 0632, New Zealand
(a division of Pearson New Zealand Ltd)
Penguin Books (South Africa) (Pty) Ltd, 24 Sturdee Avenue, Rosebank,
Johannesburg 2196, South Africa

First published in the United States of America by Viking,
a division of Penguin Young Readers Group, 2007
Published by Speak, an imprint of Penguin Group (USA) Inc., 2008
The first section of this book appeared in slightly different form in *Witpunk*,
edited by Claude Lalumière and Marty Halpern, Four Walls Eight Windows, 2003

3 5 7 9 10 8 6 4

THE LIBRARY OF CONGRESS HAS CATALOGED THE VIKING EDITION AS FOLLOWS:
Murphy, Pat, date—
The wild girls / Pat Murphy.
p. cm.
Summary: When thirteen-year-old Joan moves to California in 1972, she becomes friends with Sarah,
who is timid at school but an imaginative leader when they play in the woods,
and after winning a writing contest together they are recruited for an exclusive
summer writing class that gives them new insights into themselves and others.
ISBN 978-0-670-06226-3 (hardcover)
[1. Creative writing—Fiction. 2. Best friends—Fiction. 3. Friendship—Fiction.
4. Family problems—Fiction. 5. Self-actualization (Psychology)—Fiction. 6. Schools—Fiction.
7. San Francisco Bay Area (Calif.)—History—20th century—Fiction.] I. Title.
PZ7.M95435Wil 2007   [Fic]—dc22   2007014830

Speak ISBN 978-0-14-241245-9

Printed in the United States of America

For wild girls everywhere
and, of course, for Officer Dave

CONTENTS

the
Wild Girls

PART ONE
THE QUEEN OF THE FOXES

1

DON'T CALL ME MOUSE

I met the Queen of the Foxes in 1972, when my family moved from Connecticut to California.

I was twelve years old. I had just graduated from sixth grade, and I didn't want to move. But my father got a new job in San Francisco. My mom said California was a great place to live. Nobody asked my brother or me what we thought about the move. So that was that: the movers came and packed up all our stuff, we drove across the country, and there I was, in a new place where I didn't know anyone.

We weren't actually in San Francisco. We were in Danville, a little suburban town about half an hour's drive from San Francisco. The town was surrounded by rolling hills, and the grass on the hills was dead and dry and brown. My mom kept saying they were the "golden hills of California," but they were really just brown.

It was a summer day, and the air conditioner wasn't working. My father was at his new job and my mom was unpacking boxes while she waited for the air-conditioner repairman to come. My brother was out somewhere, trying to avoid helping Mom, I think.

We were in the kitchen. When I dropped a glass tumbler and it shattered on the linoleum floor, she told me that I'd helped quite enough.

"Joan, why don't you go out and explore the neighborhood," she said, looking up from an open box. There was an edge in her voice.

While we were packing to move and while we were driving across the country, my mom kept talking about what a great place California was, about how we would really like it there. She kept acting cheerful, like this was a wonderful adventure. But that was completely fake. I didn't believe any of it.

Now we were in California and it was too hot and there were too many boxes to unpack. At least now she wasn't pretending to be cheerful all the time.

So when she told me to go out and explore, I didn't argue. I went through the family room and out the sliding-glass door into the backyard.

Our yard in Connecticut had had lots of places to sit in the shade and read. There was a mulberry tree with a tire swing hanging from it. My mom had a big garden filled with flowers and vegetables.

This yard was nothing like that. It was a square of tired-looking grass bordered by a high wooden fence that blocked my view in all directions. From next door, I heard a splash and some kids shouting: one of our neighbors had a swimming pool.

If my mom had been there, she probably would have told me to go over and introduce myself to the kids— maybe we could all play together. But my mom wasn't there, and I didn't feel like meeting anyone new.

Our new house was on the edge of a development on the outskirts of town. I opened the gate in the back fence and looked out at a dirt road that ran alongside a set of old railroad tracks. On the far side of the tracks was an orchard—rows of trees with dark, rough trunks and smooth, pale branches. The real-estate agent had told my mom it was a walnut orchard.

If I turned right, the dirt road would lead me into the main part of town, which was about a mile away. If I turned left, the road would lead away from town, into unknown territory.

I stood by the gate for a moment, and then heard another splash from our neighbors' pool, off to the right. I turned left.

For a hundred yards or so, the dirt road ran parallel to our neighbors' back fences. Then the road left the housing development behind. To my right were the railroad tracks and the walnut orchard; to my left, another orchard and an open field. A little way farther along, the road and the railroad tracks crossed a small bridge over a creek.

I walked down the dirt road, kicking at stones. The road was deserted; I hadn't seen anyone since I left the

If it was hot anybody she want to go in the pool

backyard. But I felt exposed on the road—I could see a long way ahead of me and a long way behind, and I knew that anyone else walking on the road could see me. I didn't want to be seen. So rather than crossing the bridge, I clambered down the embankment to walk along the creek.

It was cooler by the water. Soft-leafed green trees shaded the gully. Moss grew on the rocks, and jays shrieked at me from the trees. Used to city parks, with their paths and neatly tended flowerbeds, I felt like I was entering the wilderness.

The creek turned, and a tiny path led up the bank, through a tangle of bushes and vines. I climbed up the path into an overgrown woody area. The path continued, leading through weeds and bushes that were taller than I was. There were some walnut trees here and there, but smaller trees and brush had grown up around them.

Through the trees and brush, I caught a glimpse of something orange—a brilliant, unnatural, Day-Glo color. I followed the path toward the color and found a small clearing where the weeds had been cut down. A large easy chair, upholstered in fabric that was a riot of orange daisies on green-and-turquoise paisley patterns, sat under a twisted walnut tree. In front of the chair was a flat-topped boulder, and on the boulder was a teapot with a broken spout. Boards had been wedged among the branches of the tree to make shelves of a sort. Haphazard and not quite level, they supported an odd assortment of items: a jar of peanut butter, a battered metal box, a china cup with a broken handle, two chipped plates, a dingy teddy bear, a metal box of Band-Aids.

I stopped where I was. This looked like someplace out of a book—like a troll's living room, like a wizard's retreat in the woods, like a place waiting for something to happen.

"What the hell are you doing here?" a kid's voice asked.

I looked up, startled. A girl dressed in ragged jeans and a dirty T-shirt sat on a low branch of the tree to my left. She was about my age. Her face was methodically streaked with red-brown clay—vertical stripes on her forehead, horizontal stripes on her cheeks. Her hair was a tangle of reddish curls, held back with a rubber band and decorated with a blue-jay feather.

"I . . . I was just looking around," I stammered.

"Who said you could come here?" she asked, her voice rising. "This is my place. Private property."

I felt my face getting hot. "Sorry. I just—"

"You think you can come poking around anywhere?"

"I said I was sorry. . . ."

"You kids from the development think you own everything."

"I didn't mean—"

"Why don't you just go back where you came from?"

"That would be fine with me," I managed to say, just before my voice broke. I turned away, feeling tears on my face. I immediately tripped over a rock and fell

why did she say immediately

hard, catching myself on my hands and one knee. When I scrambled to my feet, the girl was standing beside me.

"Who the hell do you think you are, anyway?" I snarled at her, trying to cover my tears with anger. "I wasn't doing anything wrong."

She was studying me, her head cocked to one side. "You haven't been here before, have you?" she asked, her voice calmer.

I shook my head. "My family just moved to this lousy neighborhood."

"Your knee is bleeding," she said. "And so's your hand. Come on and sit down. I've got some Band-Aids."

I sat in the easy chair, and she washed my cuts with water from the creek, carried in the china cup. While she dabbed at my scraped knee with a wet bandana and put Band-Aids on my injuries, she explained that some kids had been there a few days before and had messed with all her stuff, pulling down the shelves and tipping over the chair. "There are some really mean kids around here," she said. "You're lucky I didn't just start throwing rocks at you. I can hide in the trees and nail a kid with a rock from thirty feet away."

"Why didn't you?"

She shrugged. "You were by yourself. I didn't want to."

"I'm by myself a lot," I said.

"Yeah? So am I."

She sat back on her heels, studying my bandaged knee. "Well, I guess you'll be okay now." She smiled then. "You asked who I am, so I guess I better tell you." She met my eyes with a steady gaze. "I'm the Queen of the Foxes."

"The Queen of the Foxes," I repeated.

"That's right—the Queen of All the Foxes." Suddenly she was on her feet. "Come on. I'll show you something cool."

There was no time for any more questions. She was heading down a narrow path through the trees, and I had no choice but to follow.

"Something cool" was a place by the creek where you could catch orange-and-black newts that had thoughtful eyes. The Queen of the Foxes caught one and handed it to me. The newt felt like cold rubber in my hand. It didn't struggle to escape. Instead, it blinked at me and then started walking with high, slow steps, as if it were still moving through water.

The Queen of the Foxes was floundering in the water and getting thoroughly muddy. At first, I stayed on the bank. I said I'd be in trouble if I got my clothes too dirty. Then she pointed out that my bleeding hand had already left smears of blood and mud on my shorts. I would already be in trouble, so I might as well have all the fun I could. So I got into the creek, too, and released the newt that she had caught for me and caught another.

Then we sat on the bank and dried out. While we were there, she painted my face with clay from the bank. War paint, she called it. I thought it was goofy, but fun. Back in Connecticut, some girls I knew had started experimenting

Does the Queen of Foxes have parents?

with makeup—painting their fingernails and wearing lip gloss. They spent a lot of time talking about which boys were cute and what was on sale at the mall. I liked catching newts and wearing war paint a lot better.

We went back to the clearing with the easy chair, and the Queen of the Foxes showed me how to make a squawking noise by blowing on a blade of grass held tight between my hands. A couple of blue jays sat in the walnut tree and scolded us for making such a racket.

"Hey, what's your name, anyway?" I asked her.

"My name?" She leaned back and looked up at the branches of the walnut tree. "You can call me Fox."

"That's not a name."

"Why not?"

"I can't tell my mom that your name is Fox. She won't believe it."

"Why do you have to tell her anything?"

"She'll ask."

"So make up something she'll like better. You call me Fox and I'll call you Mouse."

"No, you won't."

"Then what should I call you?"

"Call me Newt," I said, thinking of the slow-moving amphibians with their thoughtful eyes. "That would be okay."

Somehow or other, the afternoon went away, and I realized that I was hungry. "Hey, I got to get going," I said. "My mom will be really pissed if I'm late for dinner."

"Ah," she said, lying back in the grass. "I don't have to worry about that. I don't have a mother."

"Yeah?" I squinted at her, but her eyes were closed and she didn't notice. As I tried to figure out what to say, I heard a man's voice calling in the distance. "Sarah! Sarah, are you there?"

She frowned. "That's my dad," she muttered. "I better go see what he wants." She ran down a different path, heading toward the sound of the voice. After a minute, I followed her.

The path led to an old white house on the edge of the woods. It wasn't like any house I'd ever seen before—there was no driveway, no yard. A dirt road that led off through the trees ended in front of the house, where a battered old sedan was parked beside an enormous motorcycle. Weeds grew in the flowerbed beside the front steps, and there was all kinds of junk near the door: a cast-iron bathtub half-filled with water, a barbeque built from an oil drum, a pile of hubcaps. The paint on the house was peeling.

Fox stood on the front porch, talking to a burly man wearing blue jeans and a black T-shirt with the sleeves torn off. They looked over and saw me standing on the edge of the woods. "This is Newt," Fox said. "Newt, this is my dad."

He didn't look like anyone's father. He needed a shave. He had three silver studs in his left ear. His dark hair was tied back with a rubber band. On his right shoulder was a tattoo, an elaborate pattern of spiraling black lines.

"How's it going, Newt?" Fox's dad didn't seem at all startled at my strange new name. "Where did you come from?"

"Uh . . . my family just moved here, Mister uh . . ."

"You can call me Gus," he said. "I don't answer to 'Mister.'"

I nodded uncomfortably. He didn't look like anyone's dad, but it still seemed strange to call him by his first name.

"I found her in the woods," Fox said. "Showed her where the newts live."

"That's good. I'm glad you found your way here." He seemed genuinely pleased. "Be nice for Fox to have some company."

I kept looking at the tattoo. I couldn't seem to keep my eyes away. I had never met anyone with a tattoo before.

He grinned, watching my face, then walked down from the porch and sat on the bottom step. "You interested in tattoos? Take a look." I studied his arm. "You can touch it if you like. It's okay."

Gingerly, I traced one of the spirals. I couldn't feel the lines on his skin: it felt like warm skin, nothing more.

"It's an ancient Celtic symbol," Gus said. "It represents constant change—transformation and rebirth. It's been good luck for me. Right after I got it, I sold my first novel."

There was a little too much there for me to absorb, but I nodded as if I understood.

After a minute, he stood up and said, "Well, it's just about time for dinner. Do you want to join us, Newt? Nothing fancy—just canned chili."

"No, thanks," I said. "I'd better go home."

"Don't forget to wash your face," he suggested.

Fox and I used the hose outside the house, and then I headed home. "See you later, Fox."

"Later, Newt. Come back tomorrow, okay? Come and have lunch."

That was how I met the Queen of the Foxes.

★　★　★

I got home right when my father got back from work and he was telling my brother that he shouldn't be sitting around watching trash on TV. I snuck up to my room and changed before anyone noticed my muddy clothes and wet shoes.

When I got downstairs, my father was complaining to my mother that it had cost too much to fix the air conditioner. My brother was watching TV again. I set the table and we had dinner.

My mother and father did not like one another much. Dinner was just about the only time they sat down together. A vague sense of tension always hung over the table, centering on my father. He was always angry—not about anything in particular, but about everything, all the time. But he pretended he wasn't angry. He was always joking, but the jokes weren't very funny.

"I see you've decided that meat is better if it's black

around the edges," he said to my mother that night. The London broil was well done, though far from black. "That's an interesting theory."

My mom laughed in a brittle way at my father's comment, ignoring the edge in his voice.

He glanced at me. "Your mother thinks that charcoal is good for the digestion," he said.

I didn't say anything. My own strategy for dealing with my father was to keep my head down. I tried not to call attention to myself. I said as little as possible.

My father turned to my brother. "So what educational shows did you watch on TV today? I'm sure you can learn a great deal from watching *The Price Is Right*."

"I didn't watch TV all day," my brother said sullenly.

"That's right," my mom said. "Mark was out all morning, exploring the neighborhood."

"I see—out looking for trouble instead of broadening your mind with television. Well, that's just fine."

Mark was three years older than I was. Once, in Connecticut, the police had picked him up for being out after curfew. My father brought that up whenever he was annoyed with Mark, and he was often annoyed.

"I'm sure there are just as many young hoodlums in this town as there were in Connecticut," my father continued. "I'm confident you'll find them."

"I met some kids down the block," Mark said. "They all belong to the country club. Can we join the country club so that I can go swimming with them?" This last question was directed to my mom.

"Swimming at the country club?" my father said. "Now isn't that nice? Maybe we need to get you a job so that you don't have so much time weighing heavy on your hands."

Mark didn't say anything. My father was talking about how young he had been when he had his first job. I noticed that Mark was staring at me, and I could feel it coming. He was going to say something to get my father off his case and onto mine. When my father paused, Mark said, "Hey, Joan, how come you always hold on to your glass when you eat? It looks stupid."

I looked down at my hands. My left hand was gripping my glass of milk tightly.

"You look like you're afraid that someone's going to try to steal your milk from you," my father said, chuckling. "Just relax. You're not living in a den of wild animals."

this chapter was about
belloging

2

A GREAT PLACE TO HIDE

The next day, my mom asked me where I'd been the day before. I told her I'd met a girl my age who lived nearby. I said that her name was Sarah and that she was interested in biology, just like I was.

I didn't bother to mention that she said she was the Queen of the Foxes, that she threw rocks at people, or that she called me Newt and I called her Fox. I figured my mom didn't really need to know all that. I said that my new friend had invited me to join her for lunch.

Just when my mom was starting to ask a bunch of questions I didn't want to answer, the phone rang. It was one of my mother's friends in Connecticut. I stood there for a minute, like I was waiting for my mother's attention, until she waved me out the door—which is what I had really been waiting for.

I went down the dirt road, along the creek, and up the little trail to Fox's clearing in the woods. Fox was curled up in the easy chair, reading a book. I had forgotten how ragged her clothes were. She had washed her face and hands and she was wearing a clean T-shirt, but the same pair of torn and grubby jeans.

"Hi," I said.

"It's too bad there aren't any hedgehogs around here," she said, as if she were continuing a conversation that we'd begun earlier. "They have them in England. They live in the gardens and the hedges." She tapped her finger on the book, and I looked over her shoulder at a picture of a spiny animal with round black button eyes. It looked kind of like a cross between a mouse and a scrub brush. "That's a hedgehog. We don't have them around here."

"It's cute," I said hesitantly.

"Foxes eat 'em," she said, grinning.

I gave her a dubious look.

"Okay," she said. "Not really. Hedgehogs have too many spines. But foxes would eat them if they could, I bet."

I didn't have a chance to reply to that. She had set the book aside. "Hey, I wanted to show you something." She was out of the chair. "Let's go." She led me off into the woods to show me where a branch of the stream ran into a culvert, a concrete tunnel that was so big that when I was standing in the stream I could barely reach the top with my outstretched arm. We waded in the stream and went into the culvert, walking through the algae-scented darkness until the mouth of the tunnel was a tiny spot of light in the distance.

"Isn't this great?" Fox's voice echoed from the cement walls.

I looked into the darkness, black and velvety, silent except for the delicate music of trickling water. It was simultaneously terrifying and inviting. In books, kids were always finding secret passages to other worlds. I didn't really believe in secret passages, but the culvert felt like it could be a secret passage if there were secret passages. "Yeah," I said. "It's great."

"Even in the middle of the afternoon, it's cool in here," Fox said. "It's a great place to hide. I don't know where it goes, but one of these days, I'm going to bring a flashlight and keep going. Then I'll find out."

I glanced toward the glimmer of light at the mouth of the culvert, then stared into the darkness again and shivered. "Okay," I said. "We could do that."

"Great. Let's go see how the newts are." She splashed in the direction of the opening and I followed, grateful to return to the heat and the light of the day.

The newts were fine, and we lay on the bank of the creek and watched squirrels run in the branches, playing what looked like an endless game of tag.

"I'll show you some secrets," she said, and she showed me a maze of tiny paths that ran through the underbrush, just big enough for us, no bigger. "Tag," she said, touching my arm, "you're it."

Then she ran away into the maze and I had to chase her, ducking under a branch, running around a corner, always staying on the path because trying to plunge through the bushes was scratchy and painful. I tagged her and then she chased me, whooping and shouting as she ran. Around and around, up this path and down that. Sometimes, I could catch a glimpse of the clearing with the easy chair. And sometimes I was deep in the bushes, concealed from the world. Around and around, like the squirrels in the branches, until I knew that the path by the broken branch led back to the clearing and that the one by a pile of rocks led back to the creek and so on.

Fox was chasing me, and she had fallen silent. I didn't know where she was. I stayed still, listening, then crept back toward the clearing. I was almost there when I heard a sound behind me. Fox dropped from a branch of a walnut tree and tagged me from behind. "You're it," she said. "Let's have lunch."

We went back to the clearing for lunch—it seemed like the most natural thing in the world to eat peanut butter on crackers under the old walnut tree.

"Are there really foxes around here?" I asked her.

"Of course."

"Can I see them?"

"Maybe sometime," she said. "They're never around during the day." She glanced down at our lunch. "They like peanut butter."

I frowned, trying to imagine a fox eating peanut butter. "So how did you get to be the Queen of the Foxes?"

She was sitting in the easy chair, and the sun shining through the leaves of the walnut trees dappled her hair. I squinted my eyes in the lazy afternoon heat, and the bright spots of light looked like jewels; the battered chair, like a throne. She tipped her head back regally, looking up into the leaves. "It started a long time ago," she said slowly. "Back when I was just a little girl."

Then she told me this story.

Once there was a woman who did not like who she was. She felt uneasy with herself, as if she did not fit inside her own body. When she looked in the mirror, she did not recognize herself. Was that her nose? Were those her eyes? They didn't seem quite right, though she could not have told you what the right nose or eyes would be.

The woman lived with her husband in a house near Golden Gate Park in San Francisco. She had a little girl who was old enough to go to school. Sometimes, the woman looked at the little girl and wondered if this little girl was really hers. She couldn't tell.

One day, when the woman's little girl was at school and her husband was at work, the woman left the key to the house on the kitchen table and walked out. She walked along a trail that led into Golden Gate Park. Even though it was in the middle of a city, Golden Gate Park was really big with lots of woods and wild places. When the woman was deep in the park, she left the trail and walked between the trees where there was no trail.

She was far from the trail when it started to rain—gently at first, and then harder, raindrops hammering against her and soaking her shirt and her jeans. She looked for a place to take shelter and found a hollow log that was large enough to crawl inside.

She crawled in on her belly. It was dry inside the log—snug and warm. She waited for the rain to stop, closing her eyes and listening

*to the water rattle against the leaves overhead, drip to the forest floor,
and trickle through dead leaves to reach the thirsty ground. Listening
to the rain, she fell asleep.*

*When she woke, she had changed. For the first time, she felt at
home in her body. The smells around her were intense and inviting—
the delicious scent of rotten leaves and grubs; the warm smell of the
squirrel that lived in the tree overhead. As she listened to the squirrel in
the branches, she could feel her ears moving to follow the sound. When
she looked at her body, she saw that she was covered with fur. She
nuzzled the long, bushy tail that curled around her paws.*

Somehow, as she slept, she had changed into a fox.

Fox shifted in the easy chair, looking at me for the first
time since she had started telling the story. "That was my
mother," she said. "I was the little girl."

I was lying on the ground, drowsing as I listened to
Fox's voice. Listening to the story about the woman turning into a fox, I had forgotten why Fox was telling it. I sat
up, staring at Fox.

"You're saying your mother turned into a fox?"

She nodded. The sunlight still dappled her hair, but
it no longer looked like jewels. She was a ragged girl sitting on a battered easy chair, watching me with a strange
intensity.

I hesitated. Maybe she was joking. Maybe she was crazy.
"That can't happen."

"It did. I left one day to go to school. When I came
back, my mother was gone."

"Maybe she just went off somewhere. Why do you figure she turned into a fox?"

Fox leaned her head against the frayed back of the chair. "About six months after she disappeared, my father and I went walking in the park just after dark. We were walking along a trail, and I saw a fox, sitting under a tree and watching us. I knew it was my mother."

"How did you know?"

"By the look in her eyes. I just knew. I asked my dad and he said that it was as good an explanation as any." She frowned, looking down at her hands. "Things weren't so great then. Dad was drinking and stuff." She looked up. "He doesn't do that anymore. Then his uncle died and left him this house and this land. So we moved out here. And after we'd been out here a month, I was sitting on the porch and I saw a fox. It stopped and looked at me."

"It wasn't the same fox," I said. "A fox couldn't get out here from San Francisco."

She shrugged. "How do you know? What do you know about foxes?"

"Not much," I admitted.

"Then how do you know it couldn't happen?"

"I guess it could," I said at last. I didn't know much about foxes, but it sure sounded like a crazy story. And I couldn't figure out if she was serious or not.

It seemed like talking about her dad might be safer than talking about her mother. "What does your dad do, anyway? How come he's at home in the middle of the day?"

"He writes stories and books. Mostly science fiction. Stuff with rockets on the cover, even when there aren't any rockets in the story."

I was silent for a moment, trying to absorb this information. I was figuring out what to say next, when Fox sat upright. "Listen," she said, her voice suddenly urgent.

In the distance, I could hear voices—some boys talking and laughing. "Come on," Fox said, jumping out of the chair. "We got to hide." I followed without question.

From a hiding place in the bushes, I could see the clearing through the branches. Three boys—my brother and two strangers—were walking down the path, talking loudly and carelessly.

"Most of the teachers are assholes," one of the strangers was saying. He was a stocky, blond boy. "Get Miss Jackson for English, if you can. She's an easy grader."

"Don't talk about it. I can't believe it's only a couple of weeks until school starts," said the other boy. He was tall, and his brown hair was greasy. "So let's stop and smoke already. No one's going to find us out here."

The blond boy had just reached the edge of the clearing. "Hey, look at this."

"All right," said the dark-haired boy.

The blond boy collapsed in the easy chair. The brown-haired boy pulled a pack of cigarettes and matches out of his pocket and lit up.

My brother was looking around at the shelves and the teapot and all Fox's stuff. "It looks like some kids' fort."

"Looks like a great place to party," said the brown-haired boy, sitting on the ground. "Bring some girls." He grinned. "No one would bother us out here."

He took a drag on the cigarette. From my hiding place, I could smell the smoke. Then he passed the cigarette to the blond boy.

"Yeah? The girls around here like to party?" my brother asked.

The brown-haired boy laughed. "Some of them are stuck up, but some are okay. Same as everywhere, I guess."

The blond boy passed the cigarette to my brother, who took one puff, then passed it back to the first boy.

I wondered where Fox was. The brown-haired guy was describing Christina, a girl who liked to party. "She's hot," he was saying. "Got a great body and she knows how to use it."

The blond boy was laughing. "Like you ever got close enough to find out."

It was weird, crouching in the bushes, watching the boys smoke and talk about school and girls. My brother wasn't acting like he did at home. There he was noisy and always acting like he was in charge, except when our dad was around. Then he just tried to stay out of the way. Here, the brown-haired kid was in charge.

I felt invisible and strangely powerful. The boys didn't know I was there. My brother didn't know I was watching him smoke. They didn't know I was listening to them.

"I gotta take a leak," the brown-haired boy said. Taking a step in my direction, he started to tug at his fly.

"Hey, this is private property." On the other side of the clearing, Fox had stepped out of the trees. "You're trespassing."

The boys all looked at her. The brown-haired boy laughed, his hand still on his fly. "Yeah, right. Well, I gotta pee, so I guess I'm going to keep on trespassing. Stick around and you'll see something you've never seen before."

Fox disappeared down the trail. The blond boy was laughing now, too. "I don't think she wants to see that, Jerry."

"Shut up, Andrew."

I backed off down the trail.

"Hey, what's that?" Jerry said, peering in my direction. "I think someone else is in there."

I was just about to run when a rock flew out of nowhere and smacked Jerry on the shoulder. And then I was running down the trail, remembering what Fox had said when I met her. *I can hide in the trees and nail a kid with a rock from thirty feet away.*

I heard Jerry crash into the bushes. I think he was chasing me, but he was too big to fit easily down the path. He was crashing around in the bushes and shouting swear words. Somewhere Fox was whooping, and I heard my brother and the blond boy cursing. The path I was on led away from the clearing, then back toward it. I scooped up some rocks from one of the piles by the trail, and when I reached a spot close to the clearing, I lobbed one at my brother. I think I hit him, but I didn't stay to watch—I was running again and there were sounds in the bushes, then another burst of cursing. One of Fox's rocks had hit home.

Fox was silent now. But I could hear crashing and cursing in the clearing. I slipped closer, moving quietly along the path. Through the bushes, I could see the boys. Andrew's arms were covered with scratches; he was picking brambles out of his T-shirt. My brother was standing at one side. He was bleeding from a cut on his cheek where a rock had hit. Jerry was pulling down the shelves in the tree and yelling obscenities. The teapot was shattered on the ground. That must have been the crash I had heard.

I heard footsteps behind me, and I shrank back into the bushes. It was Gus, coming down the path from the house. He looked large and angry.

"Now you've done it," Andrew said. He was out of the chair and starting to run away, but Gus was fast. He had one hand on the back of Andrew's T-shirt and the other on my brother's shoulder. Jerry was gone, running down the path and into the woods.

"Hey, let go," Andrew whined. "We weren't doing anything."

Gus had looked a little scary when I met him, and he had been smiling then. He wasn't smiling now. He looked around at the shelves on the ground, the broken teapot, the plates and cups scattered in the weeds, and the cigarette butt near the chair. "The evidence is against you, kid." His voice was all the more frightening, because it was low and steady. "You've been screwing with my daughter's stuff. And it looks like you've been playing with matches."

"That was Jerry," Andrew said. "We didn't do anything."

"I don't like kids messing around on my property," Gus continued, as if Andrew hadn't said anything. "I think your parents might be interested to know about all this. Maybe talking to them would be the best way to make sure this doesn't ever happen again."

Andrew was going on about how they hadn't been doing anything. I'd never seen my brother look so pale and miserable, not even when my father was ragging on him. I couldn't just leave him there.

Reluctantly, I left the safety of the bushes and stepped into the clearing. "Hey, Gus," I said hesitantly.

He glanced at me, still frowning. "You all right?"

"Yeah. Um . . ." I jerked my head at Mark. "That's my brother Mark. Um . . ." I looked at Mark, then at Gus, and then at the ground. "Maybe you could let him go?"

"Your brother, huh?" He stared at Mark and then at Andrew. "Hey, Sarah, get your ass out here, will you?" His tone had softened a little.

Fox stepped out of the trees on the far side of the clearing.

"What happened here?" Gus asked.

"They were trespassing. When I told them to leave, that kid that ran away said he was going to pee on my stuff. So we started throwing rocks at them."

"We didn't know we were trespassing," Andrew said. "We were just taking a shortcut and—"

"Do yourself a favor and shut up," Gus said.

Andrew stopped talking, and Mark didn't say anything.

"That's better," Gus said in a conversational tone. "I was out making trouble before you were born, so don't even think about lying to me. You thought you'd found a great place to hang out and smoke, where no one would bother you. By now, maybe you're thinking this isn't such a great place after all. Have you figured that out?"

Andrew didn't say anything.

"I won't ever come here again," Mark said.

Gus nodded. "Okay." He turned to Andrew. "How about you?"

"We weren't doing anything really," Andrew started saying. "We just . . ."

I saw Gus's hand tighten its grip on Andrew's T-shirt, and Andrew stopped talking. Then he said, "I won't ever come back here. And I don't smoke—not usually. Jerry wanted to smoke, that's all."

"All right," Gus said. "I believe you. Now, before you leave and never come back, you're going to help me put these shelves back in the tree, okay?"

Mark and Andrew nodded. Gus let them go. For a minute, I thought they were going to run, but then my brother turned toward the tree. They helped Gus put the shelves back while Fox and I stayed at the edge of the clearing, watching.

"All right," Gus said when they were done. "Now get the hell out of here."

The boys walked to the edge of the clearing and then started running.

"They won't be back anytime soon," Fox said gleefully. "We showed them."

Fox walked across the clearing to her dad's side; I stayed where I was, waiting for him to start the lecture that I knew was coming. We shouldn't have started trouble; we shouldn't have been looking for a fight; we shouldn't have thrown any rocks. Everything we did was wrong.

Gus didn't say anything for a moment, then he looked down at Fox. "Next time, come and get me," he said. "It's not a good idea to throw rocks at people."

"I didn't want to bother you," she said. "We were doing okay."

He shook his head. "Next time, come get me," he repeated. "I know you're tough, but I don't want you throwing rocks at people. And if I'm not around, just let trespassers be."

Fox didn't say anything.

"You hear me?" he said.

"Okay," Fox said. "I guess so."

He put his hand on her shoulder for a second. "You all right?"

"Yeah."

Gus nodded. "Well, I needed a break anyway. But I'd better get back to work."

As lectures go, it wasn't much of a lecture. He headed back for the house. I stared after him, then looked at Fox. "You know, your dad's not like any dad I've ever met."

She grinned. "Yeah, I know." Then she glanced in the direction the boys had run. "They won't be back."

"My brother was plenty scared. I could tell."

"You've got a good arm," she said. "You hit your brother good."

"Yeah." I wasn't sure how I felt about that.

"Don't you like your brother?"

I shrugged, feeling uncomfortable. "He was okay when we were little, but now he acts like a jerk most of the time."

She nodded. "How come you asked Gus to let him go?"

"I don't know. It seemed like he was already scared enough. And if my father found out that he'd been smoking . . ." I stopped, unable to describe how awful that would be. "It would be really bad."

Fox continued studying me. "A lot of girls wouldn't throw rocks at boys," she said.

I nodded, thinking about those girls in Connecticut who wore makeup and talked about which boys they wanted to date. They acted really stupid around boys, giggling all the time.

I had never been comfortable with any of that. I mean—I had a brother. I knew that boys weren't anything magical or wonderful. Some of the boys in our class were nicer than others, but I didn't think any of the boys were really cute or "to die for" like some of the girls said. I didn't want to go on a date with any of the boys I knew. I supposed that someday I'd get married and all that, but not for a long, long time, and I was just as happy about that.

"I know what you mean," I said. " I know a lot of girls that get really stupid around boys. I don't do that."

Fox nodded. "Yeah. I asked my dad about that. I asked him why girls in my class were acting goofy around boys."

"What did he say?"

"He said some guys act really stupid around girls, too."

"But he didn't say why they do it?"

"Not really. He just said it was a bad idea."

We spent the rest of the afternoon throwing rocks at the tree, just to improve our aim.

My brother was waiting for me in the backyard when I got home. He was sitting in one of the lawn chairs, not doing anything. I stopped just inside the gate. He sat there, gnawing on his lip and looking at me. The cut on his cheek had stopped bleeding and he'd washed his face. Now it just looked like a scratch, nothing to make a fuss about.

"I ought to clobber you for throwing rocks at me," he said.

I stayed by the gate, ready to run. "I got Gus to let you go."

He just kept staring at me. "So how do you know that guy?"

"He's my friend's dad."

"Andrew says he's some kind of crazed biker. He lives in this junky old house in the orchard. Andrew says he's dangerous and we should report him to the cops."

"If you did that, he'd tell the cops you were smoking and knocking stuff down."

Mark nodded. "Yeah. I guess so."

I thought about Gus's tattoo and the motorcycle in the yard. "Fox says he writes science-fiction books," I said. "He's really an okay guy."

Mark blinked at me, startled. "He writes science-fiction books?"

I nodded. When Mark wasn't watching TV, he was reading comics or science fiction. "That's what Fox says."

"Who's Fox?"

"My friend." I started for the back door.

"Hey, Joan?" he said. He was leaning forward in the chair, and his hands were in fists.

I stopped. "Yeah?"

"Thanks for asking him to let me go."

I stared at him. My brother never thanked me for anything. "Yeah. Okay."

"You won't tell Dad about any of this, right?"

I looked at him as if he were crazy. Tell Dad about Fox,

about Gus, about anything I was doing? No way. "I'm not saying anything."

"Okay." Looking relieved, he leaned back in his chair. "You know, Andrew says that girl is nuts. Everyone at school makes fun of her."

I could imagine Fox at school. She wouldn't fit in at all. She didn't look right, didn't act right. She belonged in the woods.

"You better be careful. You hang out with her, and everyone will figure you for a dweeb, too. Course, there's nothing new there." His voice was relaxing as he made fun of me. I turned away and went inside to wash up for dinner.

I think the topic was friendship,

3

OWLS AND FOXES

My mom asked a lot more questions about my new friend. I said that her father was a writer, and my mom seemed to think that was interesting.

She said she wanted to meet Sarah and her father. Every morning for the next few days, she planned to walk over to Sarah's house with me. I wasn't wild about that idea. I didn't know what my mom would think of Fox— or what Fox would think of my mom. Somehow I didn't think Gus would match my mom's idea of what a writer would look like.

Fortunately my mom was really busy. She was unpacking; she was calling the school to make sure we were enrolled; she was making curtains. Something always prevented her from joining me: a delivery was scheduled; someone called; she had to run an errand. Something always came up. One way or the other, I went to Fox's house alone.

My mom kept asking me to get Sarah's phone num-

ber so that she could call and introduce herself to Sarah's
parents. I meant to do it; I really did. But when I got over
to Fox's, I always forgot. Fox always had something going on: we were figuring out how to build a tree house,
or we were looking at one of Gus's books about edible
wild plants and trying to find some down by the creek, or
we were reading about squirrel behavior and watching the
squirrels play tag in the trees. We were busy, and somehow
I never remembered.

It was working just fine until Saturday morning, when
my mom announced that we were going over to the neighbors' for a barbeque that afternoon.

"But I was going to Sarah's," I said.

"You can't spend all your time with Sarah," my mom
said. "Mrs. Gordon wants to welcome us to the neighborhood, and I think that's very nice." Mrs. Gordon was the
realtor who had sold my parents our house. She lived next
door.

"But Sarah's expecting me," I said.

"Why don't you call her and tell her that you can't
come? I'm sure she'll understand."

"I don't have her phone number. I have to go to her
house."

"If you go over there," my mom said, "I'm sure you
won't be back in time for the barbeque. But maybe they're
in the phone book. What's her father's name?"

"His name is Gus," I said. "I don't know his last name."

The Dipsticks up for the mom

My mom gave me an exasperated look. "I don't have time to walk over there with you," she said. "I wish you had remembered to get that phone number."

"I have to go over to Sarah's," I said. "We have plans."

Just then my father came into the kitchen to get some coffee. He frowned at me. "Your plans will have to wait, Joan," he said. "Your mother has arranged this barbeque, and we all have to be there. Isn't that right?"

The last comment was to my mom. I could tell by the way my father said it that he wasn't happy about going to the barbeque, either. He was unhappy, and that meant everyone was going to be unhappy.

"It'll be fun," my mom said brightly. "You'll like the Gordons." It wasn't clear whether she was talking to me or to my father. Neither one of us responded. My father turned away, taking his coffee to the living room where he could read the morning paper.

"Cindy Gordon is just your age," my mom told me. "And Mrs. Gordon is the leader of the local Girl Scout troop. I told her that you were a Girl Scout back in Connecticut."

I must have frowned, because she asked, "Why are you making such a terrible face?"

"I . . . uh . . . I don't know if I want to be a Girl Scout now," I said hesitantly. "I mean, being a Girl Scout was fine when I was a little kid, but I don't think—"

"Mrs. Gordon says that the troop goes camping and river rafting," my mom interrupted. "It'll be great fun.

And Girl Scouts will help you make friends. I told Mrs. Gordon that I'd be able to help her with the troop."

My mom always seemed to think I needed help making friends. Back in Connecticut, she had been assistant leader of the Girl Scout troop, which meant that I couldn't have quit the Girl Scouts even if I wanted to. Our troop sold lots of cookies and did lots of crafts and planted a community garden; that was my mom's project.

"I can make friends without the Girl Scouts," I said. "I've already made one friend."

"And when you get to know Cindy, you'll have two friends," my mom said.

My mom was determined that we were going to the Gordons that afternoon and that I would join the Girl Scouts. There was no escape. I couldn't go to Fox's.

The Gordons had a built-in pool with a big deck around it. Cindy Gordon was my age—a slender girl with braces and short blonde hair. Her brother Andrew was the blond boy I had seen with my brother in the woods.

Cindy and I sat on lawn chairs on one side of the pool. Andrew and Mark were swimming; our parents were on the other side of the pool.

"Do you miss all your friends in Connecticut?" she asked me. "I'd hate to move."

"It's been okay," I said. I didn't tell her that I didn't have any really good friends in Connecticut. There were kids I hung out with, but no real friends. I liked to read and I did well in school. That made me suspect.

"What have you been doing since you moved?"

"Reading. Hanging out. Not much." I didn't mention Fox. It seemed unlikely that Cindy knew her. I studied the ice in my glass of soda.

"Are you going to be joining the Girl Scout troop?"

I shrugged. "I don't know."

"My mom's the leader," she said. "We went white-water rafting last year."

"Yeah?"

She told me about their raft trip down the Stanislaus River, and it sounded all right. "That sounds better than my troop back in Connecticut," I told her. I glanced over at my mom, but she wasn't listening. "We did a lot of art projects."

"Mostly, we go on hikes and stuff like that," Cindy said. "Sometimes we do community projects, like picking up litter. We had a paper drive to raise money for our trip. We had a couple of really good parties last year."

It didn't sound too bad, I thought. And Cindy was okay.

We went swimming and lay in the sun to dry out. Mr. Gordon barbequed hamburgers and hot dogs, and we had watermelon for dessert. Even my dad seemed to relax a little. It would have been fun, if I hadn't been thinking about Fox.

We left the Gordons' house at around six o'clock. I wanted to go to Fox's then, but my mom said it was too late for me to go wandering off. "You can go see Sarah to-morrow," she said. "And next time get her phone number so we won't go through this again."

I went to bed at my usual time, but I couldn't fall asleep. I heard my parents talking in the living room—my mom was going on about how nice the Gordons were, and my father wasn't saying much. Then I listened to the sound of canned laughter as my father watched some late-night talk show on TV. Finally, he turned off the TV and went to bed, but I lay awake, wondering whether Fox had missed me that afternoon.

I felt itchy and restless and finally I couldn't stay in bed any longer. I got up quietly, got dressed, and snuck through the quiet house and out the sliding glass door into the backyard. I hurried out the back gate, afraid that my parents would catch me.

I followed the dirt road toward Fox's. The first stretch of dirt road wasn't too bad. Light spilled over the fences from people's backyards, and I could kind of see where I was going. But then I turned off the road into the woods, where it was dark. There was a half moon, but only a little light filtered through the trees.

The woods sounded different at night. Frogs were croaking in the creek, and I kept hearing things rustling in the bushes. I heard an owl calling, a low mournful hoot-ing that sent a chill up my spine. Even though I knew the way, I kept thinking I must have lost the path. I couldn't help thinking about zombies and high-school students out looking for trouble. In my mind, the two seemed equally threatening.

As I walked along the narrow path, the bushes kept brushing against me. Every time a twig caught on my shirt, it felt like the zombies were grabbing me. It was a relief to get to the clearing, but it was weird being there alone in the middle of the night.

Moonlight shone down through the branches of the walnut tree and the boards that served as makeshift shelves, casting a tangle of shadows. The owl called again, and I just about jumped out of my skin. Then I saw something move in a shadow by the tree, and I froze right where I was.

A fox stepped from the shadows. In the moonlight, her fur was silvery gray; her eyes were golden. She sat down and neatly curled her tail around herself, studying me as if she were coming to some sort of decision. Then she stood up and trotted away down the path toward Fox's house.

I hesitated, and then followed. As I got closer, I could hear the *tap-tap-tap* of a typewriter.

I climbed the stairs to the porch. The light in the kitchen window was on. Gus was sitting at the kitchen table, typing on a manual typewriter. As he typed, he stared intently at the paper in the machine. As I watched, he stopped typing. I think he had reached the end of a sentence. He leaned back in his chair, picked up the bottle of Coca-Cola from the table beside him, and took a long drink. Then he set the bottle down and kept staring at the paper.

I hesitated, staring in through the screen door. For a minute, I thought about turning around and going home. Fox was probably already asleep. But I didn't want to go through the dark woods alone again.

A moth fluttered against the screen, trying to get to the light. Gus glanced at the door and frowned. "Who's that?" he said. "Newt, is that you?"

"Yeah."

He got up and opened the door. "What are you doing here so late?"

I stepped into the kitchen, glad to be leaving the darkness outside. "I came to see Fox."

"She's asleep. You should be asleep, too."

I hadn't been in Fox's house before. The kitchen sink was filled with dirty dishes, but that wasn't what caught my attention. There were bookshelves on every wall—some crammed with books, others with papers. It seemed so weird: bookshelves in the kitchen.

"What's going on?" Gus asked.

"I wanted to talk to Fox. Is she . . . is she mad at me?"

Gus sat down at the kitchen table. He gestured to a chair where I could sit. "She was upset that you didn't come by. And we didn't have your phone number, so we couldn't call you."

"My mom made me go to a barbeque at the next-door neighbors' house. I wanted to call, but I didn't have your phone number. I didn't even know your last name, so I couldn't look it up. My mom said it was too late to come

IS FOX A FOX?

out here, so I had to wait and sneak out. It was really scary in the woods, but I kept going. I saw a fox . . ."

I was talking really fast. I don't know exactly why, but I felt like crying. Maybe because I was thinking about Fox being mad; maybe because I had been really scared in the woods. Gus held up a hand, stopping me in mid-sentence.

"Relax, Newt," he said. "Slow down. Take a deep breath." He watched me for a moment. Without getting up, he reached over to a bookcase and grabbed a spiral-bound notebook and a pencil. "Here. Write it down."

I was so startled that I did what he said. I took a deep breath and then another. The feeling that I was about to cry went away.

I looked at the notebook on the table in front of me. "Write it down?"

"Yeah. Write a note that explains what happened. I'll make sure Fox gets it."

"Why can't you just tell her?"

"I could. But it wouldn't be the same. If you write it, it'll be like you're talking to her." He sipped his Coke, leaning back in his chair. "If I told her, I'd say it in my words. You should say it in your own words. That's important."

He seemed pretty determined. If I wanted Fox to know what happened, I'd have to write it down. "Okay," I said reluctantly.

I sat at the kitchen table and wrote a long note to Fox about how I couldn't call because I didn't know her phone number and about how my mom wouldn't let me go and about sneaking out after dark and about seeing the fox in the clearing.

While I was writing, Gus started typing again. I kept writing. I wrote about how I had wanted to come to tell her. I wrote about how I knew she was mad at me and I was sorry about that.

Finally I tore the pages from the notebook and held them out to Gus. He looked up from his typewriter.

"Good," he said. "Now could you write your phone number on the note so that Sarah has it? Even wild girls in the woods like you two can take advantage of modern technology."

I wrote my phone number at the bottom of the note, and I handed him the notebook and the note. He set the note on the table and opened the notebook to the first page, where he wrote down a phone number. "There's our phone number," he said, handing me the notebook. "Now you keep that notebook and use it when you want to write down other stuff."

"What kind of stuff?"

"Stuff that happens," he said. "Stuff that you're scared of. Stuff that you make up. Sometimes it helps to write stuff down."

I frowned. "I don't see how writing something down would help with anything."

He glanced at the page in his typewriter and shrugged. "Maybe it's just me. But when you write something down, you have to think it all the way through. Sometimes, I'm not even sure how I feel about something until I write a story about it. I figure it out while I'm writing the story."

He was talking softly, his eyes on the typewriter. I wondered what he was writing a story about. What was he trying to figure out?

"Or maybe you want to keep a journal," he said. "I started keeping a journal when I was around your age. You might want to give it a try." Then he shrugged. "It's up to you. Just keep the notebook and maybe it'll be useful. Come on—I'll walk you home."

I carried the notebook under my arm and followed Gus through the woods.

Now there was nothing to be afraid of. The shadows were just shadows. The owl hooted, and Gus hooted back. He told me it was a great horned owl, out hunting for mice. The rustling noises were just birds and mice. I didn't worry about zombies or high-school students. Neither one would dare attack Gus.

He left me at the gate in the back fence.

＊　＊　＊

When I went back the next day, I found Fox in the clearing, sitting in the easy chair. She looked up when she saw me. "Hey, Fox," I said. "I'm sorry I had to go to that stupid barbeque yesterday."

"My dad told me that you came out here. He gave me your note."

"He said you were mad at me."

"I was," she said. "But he told me that not all parents are as understanding as he is. Some parents push their kids around."

"He got that right."

"Yeah. He told me he gave you a notebook, so you could keep a journal."

"Yeah."

"You going to do it?" she asked.

"I don't know. Maybe." That wasn't quite true. The night before, when I got home, I had written a bunch of stuff about going to Fox's house. I knew that I'd keep writing in the notebook. But I wasn't sure I wanted to admit it.

"I've been writing in a journal since I was nine," she said.

I nodded, relieved to find out that she didn't think it was a stupid idea.

"Come on," she said. "Let's go to the tunnel."

"The tunnel" was the culvert. Sometimes, we walked deep into the darkness and Fox made up stories: we were the first explorers in the world's deepest cave; we were rebels, hiding in the sewers of Paris; we were traveling to the center of the earth, where there were still dinosaurs.

That day, Fox didn't make up a story. We just walked into the darkness, the cold water squishing in our sneakers as we walked. We were deep in the culvert when Fox stopped. I bumped into her in the darkness. Then she said,

"You said in your note that you saw the fox. What did you think of her?"

"She was beautiful."

"Yeah, she is."

I wished I could see Fox's face. She sounded strange—her voice tight and strained.

"What did her eyes look like?"

"Like . . . like she knew what I was thinking."

"Yeah." For a moment, Fox was silent. Then she said, "My mom was beautiful. Her hair was the color of fox fur. Kind of rusty red-brown."

I hesitated. "Do you really think she became a fox?" I asked cautiously.

A long silence, then she whispered in the darkness. "Sometimes, you gotta believe something crazy. Because all the other things you could believe hurt too much." In the darkness, I could hear Fox's breathing. I could hear water trickling somewhere. "I mean, I could try to believe something else. Like she just ditched my dad and me and went off with some other guy. But I think it would be really cool to turn into a fox. I could see why you'd want to do that. And I like thinking of her as a fox, living out in the woods. So that's what I believe."

"Yeah," I said. "I can see that." It did make a kind of crazy sense. I groped in the darkness and took her hand. "Okay—then I'll believe it, too."

"Hey, let's go and see the newts," Fox said, leading the way out of the darkness.

When I got home, I gave my mom Fox's phone number. The next morning, she told me she had talked with Gus.

"I'll be joining you for lunch today," my mom said. "Gus invited me over."

I stared at her, speechless.

"Won't that be nice?" she said.

That wasn't the word I would have used. "I guess so," I said.

I told my mom that I'd come back to show her the way to Fox's, and then I fled. I rushed over to Fox's and found Gus and Fox in the kitchen, unloading grocery bags.

"Hello, Newt," Gus said. "What has you in such a panic?"

"You invited my mom to lunch," I said.

"Sure," he said. "She wants to check us out."

I looked around the kitchen. The sink was still full of dirty dishes. Papers overflowed the bookshelves. The paint on the ceiling was peeling. I looked at Fox in despair, and she shrugged. I knew that my mom would take one look at all that and say that I couldn't ever come back. Gus clearly didn't have a clue.

"There's nothing to worry about," Gus said. "We'll have a picnic. Just relax and help Fox make a fruit salad."

I shook my head. Like I said: not a clue.

Fox was dressed in a clean T-shirt and shorts, and her hair was tied back in a ponytail. That was good, anyway.

Is Joans ?
momfancy!

"My dad says we need to make a good impression," she told me.

I helped Fox chop up apples and oranges and bananas for a fruit salad. Gus made tuna sandwiches and washed all the dishes in the sink. That was good, but the bookshelves were still overflowing and the paint was still peeling. I knew my mom would hate it.

Fox went back to my house with me. My mom had made chocolate chip cookies, and the house smelled great. I realized, when I smelled the cookies baking, that this was the first time she had done that since my dad had announced we were moving. Before that, she used to make a big batch of cookies or brownies every few weeks. "I thought I might bring some cookies for dessert," she said.

"That would be great," Fox said. "They smell really good."

My mom smiled. "You must be Sarah."

Fox nodded and politely shook my mom's hand. I could tell that she was on her very best behavior.

My mom offered to drive, but I didn't know how to get to Fox's house by car. So my mom followed us down the dirt road and along the narrow trail through the bushes and the clearing to Fox's house. My mom got burrs all over her pants legs from the weeds and mud on her shoes from the path by the creek.

Gus had set up a card table under one of the walnut trees near the house. He had covered it with a red table-

cloth and set it with paper plates. It looked pretty good—
as long as you ignored all the junk in the yard nearby.

I glanced at my mom. She was studying the rusting car,
the old bathtub, the pile of hubcaps, the motorcycle, and
all the rest of the stuff. She wasn't smiling anymore. Her
eyes were narrow and her mouth was in a hard, straight
line.

Just then, Gus came onto the porch, carrying a plastic
pitcher of lemonade. He was wearing a Hawaiian shirt,
and the sleeves covered the tattoo on his shoulder. His
long dark hair was neatly combed back and he wasn't wearing any earrings. He still didn't look like anyone's dad, but
he looked a little less like the leader of a motorcycle gang
than usual.

"Hello," he called to my mom. "I'm Gus, Sarah's father. You must be Joan's mom. Welcome to our humble
home."

My mother had started smiling in a determined sort
of way, the kind of smile she put on when she didn't really
mean it.

"I'm so glad to meet you at last." Gus crossed the yard
and set the pitcher on the table. "It's been very nice having
your daughter come to visit."

Gus seemed genuinely happy to see my mom. He smiled
and poured her a glass of lemonade.

"I brought some chocolate chip cookies," my mother
said stiffly, holding out the plate.

Gus took the plate from her hand and grinned. "Wow! I

haven't had homemade chocolate chip cookies in years."

"Your wife doesn't like to bake?"

"My wife . . . isn't with us anymore."

"Oh, I'm so sorry." She glanced at Fox, at Gus, at the house—and I could see her reconsidering the situation. Her face softened a little. "I didn't realize . . ."

Gus set the cookies on the table. "Please sit down," he said. "It's a beautiful day for a picnic."

We sat in the shade and ate lunch. Fox and I pretty much kept quiet while my mom and Gus talked.

Gus asked my mom how she liked California, and she talked about missing her garden in Connecticut. It was funny—I knew that I missed the garden and the big backyard, but I hadn't thought about how she must miss it.

Gus talked about his garden: a riot of tomatoes and squash that bore little similarity to the carefully weeded rows of vegetables that my mom grew. He said that his uncle, who had left him the house, always had a big garden. He told her which nearby nursery was the best.

Gradually my mom's smile shifted from a stiff, forced, company smile to something more genuine. She asked questions about Gus's writing, and he told her the titles of some of his books. "Mostly science fiction," he said, "which isn't everyone's cup of tea." Then he laughed. "I've also written some romance novels under a pseudonym." After some coaxing, he told her the pseudonym.

On the way home, my mom was quiet. That made me nervous. I didn't know what she was thinking.

Finally, I said, "I know their house is kind of a mess." I figured I was better off mentioning it before she did.

"It is," my mother agreed. "Needs painting and cleaning up." Then she frowned. "It must be hard for him to be raising a daughter by himself," she said. "And I don't imagine writing science fiction brings in all that much money."

"I guess it doesn't," I said. I was thinking about Fox's tattered clothes. They had seemed like the right sort of thing for a wild girl to be wearing. But listening to my mom, I wondered if there were other reasons that all her clothes were old.

My mom didn't say anything for a few minutes. We were walking down the dirt road and she was kind of staring off into the distance, as if she was thinking about something else. "My folks never had much money when I was growing up," she said at last. "I know how hard that can be."

She glanced at me. "You know, I wonder if those jeans that you've outgrown would fit Sarah. She's a little smaller than you are."

"I can ask," I said. And I knew that things would be okay.

RETURN OF THE QUEEN
OF THE FOXES

A week later, school started. I'd always been good in classes—I did well on tests; I got good grades. When I was in fourth grade, I got a C in math, because I thought arithmetic was boring. From my father's reaction, you would have thought it was the end of the world. He immediately bought flash cards. Every night, he quizzed me on the multiplication table. He insisted on checking my homework over, and I had to stand there while he did it, terrified that I'd get something wrong. It was horrible, and I decided that it would be a lot easier to get good grades than to deal with the consequences of getting bad ones.

I was a good student. I did my best to know all the answers, but I usually sat quietly, volunteering as little as possible. Life was easier that way.

On the first day of school in California, it was pretty clear that this school was going to be a lot easier than my school back in Connecticut. Last year in Connecticut, everyone in my sixth-grade class had to write reports on _why Does Fox get dressed for school?_

aspects of the Russian revolution. I wrote about Rasputin. In seventh-grade history in California, the teacher was talking about how we would build a replica of the Parthenon from sugar cubes. I figured I could handle that.

The teacher was calling roll in my English class when I saw Fox in the back row. I almost didn't recognize her. Her face was clean, and she was wearing a blouse and a skirt.

I'd never seen her in a skirt before. Even then, she looked out of place. She was smaller than most of the girls. Her hair was tied back, but frizzy bits were escaping. I kept glancing her way, but she didn't look back. She was frowning and she looked uncomfortable.

The teacher, Mrs. Parsons, was a fluttery woman with wispy hair and a high, breathless voice. That first day, she read us a poem about daffodils and asked us what we thought of it. I didn't think much of it. It was kind of fluffy, like Mrs. Parsons.

When class was over, I hurried to catch Fox on her way out. "Hey, Fox. How's it going?"

She glanced at me, not smiling. "Around here, my name's Sarah."

"Okay. And mine's Joan."

"Look—I gotta go," she said. She was walking quickly, and I had to hurry to keep up. She hugged her books to her chest as if she were cold.

"What's the matter?" I said. "Where are you going?"

She didn't slow down. "I've got some stuff to do."

*was not
Fox not
at Joan's*

"Hey, Joan!" I turned and saw Cindy Gordon and another girl standing at a nearby locker.

I touched Fox's arm. "Come on," I said. "That's Cindy Gordon. She lives next door to me. Let's go say hi." I walked toward them, but when I got there, Fox wasn't with me. I saw her back as she headed away down the corridor.

"Hi, Cindy," I said.

"Hi, Joan. This is Sue. Sue, this is Joan. She moved in next door to me."

Sue was staring after Fox. "Do you know that girl?" Sue asked me.

"Yeah. Why?"

She glanced at Cindy but didn't answer my question.

Cindy closed her locker and said, "Joan just moved here from Connecticut. She's going to join the Girl Scout troop." She looked at me. "We're going to the cafeteria to get some lunch. Want to come?"

Fox was no longer in sight. I shrugged uncomfortably. "Sure. I guess so."

I ate a hamburger at a table with Cindy and Sue and a couple of their friends. They asked me a few questions about Connecticut, but mostly they talked about the classes they were in together and what their teachers were like.

They were good girls, smart girls, girls who got good grades. A couple of them were in the Senior Girl Scout troop, and they all told me about the white-water rafting trip they'd gone on. Sue said they wanted to go on a horse-packing trip next summer.

One of the girls, a redhead named Colleen, was in my English class. She told me that Mrs. Parsons was an easy grader and that a few years ago she had started crying when she was reading a sad story to her class. "My sister was in that class," Colleen said. "She said it was really weird."

I walked to science class with Cindy and Sue. We sat together in the front of the room. The teacher, Mr. Mc-Farland, was a tall, skinny guy wearing plaid pants and a shirt with a pocket protector. He talked for a while, and then asked us to pair up with someone to be lab partners. When everyone was milling around, trying to find a partner, I saw Fox at the back of the class, standing alone. I left Cindy and Sue, who had paired up immediately, and went over to her.

"Hey," I said to her. "Want to be partners?"

She looked at me, frowning a little. "Don't do me any favors."

I frowned back. "What's with you?" I said, very quietly. "Why are you acting so weird?"

"Didn't your new friends tell you? I *am* weird."

I followed her gaze. Cindy and Sue carefully looked away when I glanced at them. Then I looked back at Fox. "Look—do you want to be lab partners or not?"

"Okay," she said reluctantly.

For the rest of class, Mr. McFarland had us taking flowers apart and looking at all the parts: the sepals, the petals, the stamen, the pistil. Fox worked with me, but she wasn't the same person that she was in the woods. She was quieter, more subdued. In the woods, she was in charge; she knew what she was doing. Here, she didn't fit.

After we were done, I went back to my seat with Cindy and Sue. At the end of class, Fox vanished into the crowd of students before I could catch up with her.

After school, as I walked home with Cindy and Sue, Sue asked me about Fox. "So how do you know Sarah?"

"I met her when I was exploring out in the orchard," I said, feeling uncomfortable because I figured that Cindy and Sue would never go wandering in the orchard by themselves for no particular reason.

"I heard that she and her father live in this junked-out house," Sue said. "Her father's really scary. He rides this big Harley and he has a tattoo."

"I've been to her house," I said slowly. "And I met her dad. He's a neat guy. He writes science-fiction books."

Sue was looking at me as if I just told her that I'd been to Mars in a UFO. "You've been to her house? Wow."

"Yeah, I've been to her house," I said, with a bit of an edge in my voice.

"Hey," Cindy said, "what did you think of Mr. Mc-Farland's pants? Weren't those wild?"

So we talked about Mr. McFarland and how weird he was. I was grateful that Cindy had changed the subject. I got the feeling that she didn't like the way that Sue was trashing Fox. But when she asked if Sue and I wanted to come over for a swim, I said I couldn't. "Gotta do some stuff at home for my mom," I said.

Cindy and Sue went off together, and I went home, changed into jeans, and headed for the clearing in the woods. Fox wasn't there. I went to her house, and Gus said she had come home and then gone out to play. He was sitting at the typewriter, and he looked up just for a minute. He seemed kind of busy.

I went to the clearing and sat in the big chair for a while, waiting. Then I checked down by the stream where we caught newts. Finally I went to the culvert.

I listened at the opening. "Fox?" I called. No answer. The water was low now, just a trickle running down the center of the culvert. There were a couple of muddy footprints on the dry cement beside the water, and they looked about the right size for Fox's feet. "Fox?" I called again.

I thought I heard someone breathing, but no one answered. So I walked into the darkness. My footsteps echoed the length of the tunnel.

It was strange, walking in the darkness by myself. Every other time I'd been there, Fox had been leading the way. It seemed darker than it had ever been before. "Fox?"

"Yeah?" Her voice was soft. She was just a little bit farther in.

"I was looking for you."

"Well, you found me."

I bumped into her. She was sitting on the side of the culvert, her feet in the water. I sat down beside her.

"You didn't wait for me after class."

"I figured you wanted to hang out with those other girls."

"You could have walked home with us," I said.

"No, I couldn't. They don't like me."

"Sure you could have. They just don't know you," I said. Even as I said it, I wondered if she was right. Cindy might accept her, but I didn't think Sue would.

Fox didn't say anything.

"You know, I'm going to have to join the Girl Scout troop. My mom wants me to. If you joined the Girl Scouts, then—"

"No thanks," she said. "That wouldn't change anything. I don't like them and they don't like me."

I sat with her in the darkness, wondering if she was right and wondering why she didn't even want to try. She was so brave when she was climbing trees and throwing rocks, but not brave at all when it came to other people.

"Forget school," she said suddenly. "Let's see how far we can go in the tunnel."

"Right now? We don't have flashlights or anything." The light of the entrance was very far away.

"Come on," she said. "I think I know where it comes out."

I followed her into the darkness, splashing through the water. She kept hurrying on ahead, in charge again and searching for adventure.

"Wouldn't this be a great place to hide a treasure if you

had one?" she was saying. "No one would ever find it in here."

The light of the entrance disappeared behind us. The air smelled stale and muddy. I kept thinking about what it would be like to be trapped in the dark forever. I could feel my heart beating faster, and it was kind of hard to breathe. I kept telling myself that we couldn't get lost—there was only one tunnel, and to get out, all we had to do was turn back. But I had a hard time believing that.

At last, after what seemed like hours, I saw a pinpoint of light ahead of us, getting bigger as we approached.

When we emerged into the sunlight, Fox was grinning. We were on the far side of the orchard; we had walked maybe half a mile underground. "Wasn't that cool?" she said.

I looked up at the sky, glad to be back in the light of day. "Yeah," I admitted. "That was kind of cool. I couldn't have done it without you," I said.

She nodded, acknowledging her position and authority. She was the Queen of the Foxes.

I predict that Fox is going to stop hagging out with Joan

5

PUPPIES, KITTENS, AND A BIG GREEN FROG

That school year, my life was divided into two worlds.

After school and on weekends, I spent as much time as I could with Fox in the woods. At school, I walked a narrow line. Sometimes, I hung out with Cindy and other girls from the Girl Scout troop, which my mom had insisted I join. And sometimes I hung out with Fox. I was still a good student—though there were times when I had to work hard to find a way to be good.

In science class one day, we walked in and found a glass aquarium tank filled with big green frogs. Mr. McFarland held a squirming frog and demonstrated to the class how to stick a needle in the back of the frog's neck and sever the spine. Then we were supposed to dissect the frog and see its beating heart.

When he asked if there were any questions, Fox raised her hand. I was surprised. She hardly ever raised her hand in class. When Mr. McFarland called on her, she said she wouldn't do it. "I'm not sticking a needle in a frog," she said.

He nodded, and said that he would kill the frog for any teams that couldn't do it themselves.

"No," she said. Her voice was shaking a little. "I won't cut up a frog if you kill it. I won't have anything to do with this." She was almost shouting at him, and he was getting a little red in the face.

"Well, I guess you'll have to talk about that with the Dean of Girls," he said stiffly. "Joan, why don't you join one of the other groups?"

All of the kids were staring at Fox. I bet most of them didn't want to kill a frog either, but Fox was the only one willing to say anything.

"I won't do it, either," I said quietly. "I guess I'd better go see the Dean of Girls, too."

Mr. McFarland looked surprised. I worked, I was quiet, and I usually got along okay with him (even if he did wear plaid pants). But I couldn't abandon Fox.

So we both went off to see Mrs. Johnson, the Dean of Girls. She was a large woman who always wore pantsuits. Her office smelled of face powder. Some of the girls said she used so much makeup that her face cracked when she smiled. But she wasn't smiling now. "Mr. McFarland says you girls are refusing to participate in class," she said, and her voice was grim.

"We aren't really refusing," I said, before Fox could say anything. "It just seems so mean to cut up a frog."

While Fox sat with her arms folded, looking miserable and stubborn, I explained what was going on. When

I talked about sticking a needle in a frog, Mrs. Johnson's frown deepened and she looked a little sick. I did a lot of talking about cruelty to animals and respect for life. By the time I was done, the Dean of Girls was sympathetic. She said she could understand what she called our "squeamishness."

Then I suggested that Fox and I do a different project. "Maybe we could keep one of the frogs in an aquarium and observe it," I suggested. "We could write a report about it."

Eventually Mrs. Johnson and Mr. McFarland agreed on that. So Fox and I did research in the library about how to take care of a frog. We figured out what the frog ate and where it lived when it wasn't stuck in our classroom. We set up an aquarium in the back of the classroom and went to the pet store to buy crickets for our frog to eat. At Gus's suggestion, we named the frog Henry, which means "ruler of a kingdom." We figured the aquarium was about as small as a kingdom could get.

Fox was really into the project. We stayed at school late a couple of days to observe Henry. Mostly, he sat in the water with his eyes just above the surface. But sometimes he flicked out his sticky tongue and caught a cricket.

While we were watching Henry, Mr. McFarland was correcting papers, but sometimes he'd come over to the tank and see how Henry was doing. I told him about the newts in the creek. Mr. McFarland told us that when he was a kid he had caught tadpoles and kept them until they turned into frogs. Fox said she wanted to try that. Mr. McFarland even found a book that showed pictures of a frog dissection, step by step, so that we could learn about frog anatomy without killing Henry. So we did okay on the test.

That all worked out fine. It was more work than just dissecting the frog like everyone else, but it was also more interesting. And Fox got a B in science rather than her usual C, which was a bonus.

In English class, I wrote poetry that I knew Mrs. Parsons would like. Stuff that rhymed, stuff about soft and fluffy things. Not too soft and fluffy, though—writing about kittens and flowers was cliché, she said, but you could write about clouds and rain and sad feelings, and she liked that. I'd always been good at figuring out what teachers liked and giving it to them. That was one reason I got good grades.

Fox just wouldn't do that, even after I explained my strategy to her. "You're writing stuff that will make her happy rather than writing stuff that you like," she told me. "Why waste your time?"

"I write what she likes, and I get As," I said. "That keeps my father off my back."

"But it's not honest," she said.

I just shrugged.

Fox shook her head and kept on writing stuff that got Cs from Mrs. Parsons. I thought Fox's writing was more interesting than mine, but it wasn't about the sort of things that Mrs. Parsons liked. Fox wrote about the junk in her front yard or the rust on the fender of her dad's car or the smell of the walnut tree in the rain or the damp darkness in the culvert.

She wouldn't take the time to make sure that everything was spelled right, and she wouldn't bother to copy every poem over so that there weren't any cross-outs. Her handwriting was awful. Mrs. Parsons took points off for spelling and for neatness, but I think the real reason that Fox got Cs was because her poems made Mrs. Parsons nervous.

When Mrs. Parsons got entry forms for a short-story contest for girls, sponsored by some organization of women writers, she gave me one. "They want imaginative stories from girls like you," she told me. "Why don't you write a story and show it to me? I can help you with it, and then we can send it in."

At lunch that day, Cindy told me that Mrs. Parsons had given her an entry form, too. "I'm going to write about going rafting," she told me earnestly. "We found litter in the river, and that made me think about nature." I nodded politely, though I couldn't imagine anything duller.

After school, I told Fox about the contest, and she gave me a hard time about it. "Are you going to write a wonderful, thoughtful story about puppies and kittens for Mrs. Parsons?" she asked me.

We were sitting on Fox's porch. The sun had come out after almost a month of rainy days. The cool air smelled of wet leaves.

"You ought to write about something that you really care about," Fox said. "My dad says that's where the best writing comes from."

I felt uncomfortable. Ever since Gus had given me the notebook, I'd been writing in it every day. In that notebook, I was honest. I wrote about what happened and how I felt. And I knew that Mrs. Parsons would hate all that stuff.

"If I do that, I won't want to show it to Mrs. Parsons."

"You don't have to show it to her. You've got the entry form. You can just send it in yourself."

"Maybe you should write something, too," I suggested.

Fox shook her head. "Yeah, right. Like they'd be able to read my writing."

"Maybe we should write something together," I said. I glanced at her. "What could we write about?"

"The wild girls," Fox said, without hesitation. "The wild girls who live in the woods."

"How did they get there?"

She was looking out into the woods, squinting a little against the sun. "One of them grew up there."

"Her mother was a fox," I said immediately. I thought about it for a moment, and then I said, "I think her father was a wizard. The wizard loved the fox and turned her into a woman, but she was never happy, so she went back to being a fox."

"Okay," Fox said slowly. "And I guess the other one came along later. She's a princess, the daughter of an evil king and a beautiful queen. She's traveling through the forest on her way to get married to an evil duke. But she runs away and finds the wild girl in the forest."

I nodded, even though I wondered a bit about the beautiful-queen part. "Okay. And then they team up and it's like Robin Hood. They steal from the rich and give to the poor."

"And all the animals in the forest are their friends."

So we decided to write a story. I didn't tell Mrs. Parsons; I didn't tell my mom. We told Gus, but he was the only one we told. He showed us where he kept his dictionary so that we could look up words, and otherwise he left us alone.

My mom asked me about the contest once, a few weeks after we'd started working on the story. "Cindy's mother tells me that she's writing a story for a young-writers contest. Don't you want to write a story?"

I couldn't tell her what Fox and I were doing. If I did, she would insist on reading it. I just said, "I'm really busy with school."

The phone rang then, and I got away.

Fox and I worked a little bit every day. The wizard, as I described him, looked pretty much like Gus. The wild girls had a tree house that perched in the branches of an old walnut tree. The queen, as Fox described her, looked a lot like my mom. The enchanted forest, where the wild girls lived, was filled with magical creatures. Water nymphs lured men to drown in streams and bogs. Trolls lived in caves on the rocky slopes where the forest met the mountains. The wizard had a talking raven.

Sometimes, Fox and I would argue about the people in the story. When we were writing the part where the princess escaped from her guards and ran away into the forest, Fox said that the beautiful queen had given the princess a magic cape that made her invisible so that she could get away.

"Why would the queen do that?" I asked.

"To help her daughter get away."

"But the queen is sending the princess off to marry the Black Duke," I said. "The queen isn't going to help her get away."

Fox shook her head stubbornly. "I think it's the evil king that wants her to marry the Black Duke. The queen would help her."

"But the queen doesn't know any magic," I said. "Where would she even get a cape of invisibility?"

"I don't know. Maybe she bought it from a traveling wizard."

We argued for a while, but Fox was really stubborn. Finally we agreed that the beautiful queen gave her daughter peasant clothes so that she could disguise herself when she escaped her guards and ran away into the enchanted forest. In the forest, she met up with the wild daughter of the wizard, and together they saved a village from an angry troll.

Fox and I worked on the story for a long time. Then

I use white out

we asked Gus to let us use his typewriter to type it up. He showed us how to use Wite-Out, this white paint you use to cover up mistakes when you type.

Finally, we were done. I read the story over three times, just to be sure. Gus took it to the copy store and made a copy. Then he gave us a big envelope and stamps, and we mailed the story in.

Until we mailed it, no one had read the story except for us. I didn't want my mom to read it. I didn't want Gus to read it. I didn't care if the judges read the story; I didn't know them and they didn't know me.

Sometimes, when I was going to sleep, I would think about the adventures of the wild girls in the woods. I would wonder what they might do next. It was like having a secret world that only Fox and I could visit.

Joan and Fox wants to be in the story

6

WAR PAINT

For a couple of days after we sent our story in, we didn't know what to do with ourselves. It was strange to be finished. We knew that the story couldn't even have reached the contest judges yet, but we kept checking the mail anyway.

For a while, we practiced reading the story aloud. Fox said we had to, because the contest winners would. I knew there was no way we would win, so I didn't see the point in worrying about practicing for something that would never happen. But reading the story was fun, so I went along with it. We figured out who would read which parts. Fox was good at voices—she could make her voice deep to be the fox girl's wizard father, or raspy and mean for the evil king.

It wasn't until a couple of months later that Mrs. Parsons asked Fox and me to stay after class. She had the strangest expression on her face—her eyes were angry, but her mouth was smiling a tight little smile. I knew we were in trouble for something, but I couldn't guess what it was.

"You girls didn't tell me you were entering the young-writer contest," Mrs. Parsons said.

"Oh." I glanced at Fox and then back at Mrs. Parsons. "We didn't want to bother you, so we just mailed it in ourselves."

She nodded, still smiling that tight little smile. "Well, congratulations. The contest organizers called me. Your story won first prize in your age group."

I stared at her, shocked. She was still talking.

"Your mother didn't even know you had entered, Joan. I called to tell her the good news."

I nodded, trying to smile. "I thought it would be a surprise."

"Oh, she was surprised. And very happy, of course. It's quite an honor. The contest organizers want you to come to San Francisco and read the story aloud at a ceremony; they'll be printing it in an anthology of stories for girls."

I looked at Fox, and she was grinning. "We won," she said. "We won. I told you we would win."

I wanted to jump up and down and hug her, but Mrs. Parsons was still talking. I wasn't really paying attention.

"I'm really looking forward to reading the story," she said. "The judges thought it was extremely imaginative and well crafted."

Of course, there was no keeping the story to ourselves

after that. Mrs. Parsons got the contest organizers to send her a copy, after I lied and said we didn't keep one. Mrs. Parsons gave a copy to my mom, and they both read it.

Mrs. Parsons had to pretend to like it, since it had won the contest. But I don't think she liked it at all. "It's very imaginative," she said. "Your metaphors are very nice." She was always talking about metaphors in class. "But I do wish you had shown it to me before you sent it in. I think I could have helped you tone it down just a little."

We let Gus read it then. He smiled afterwards. "It's got the raw power of adolescence," he said. "Great stuff." And then, when I was heading home that afternoon, he said, "Give my regards to the evil king."

My mom was very happy that we had won. She read the story and said she liked it. Then she started making plans for the ceremony. She talked to Gus on the phone. "I thought I'd take the girls shopping for some clothes," she told him brightly. "It's such a special occasion, and I know they'll want to look nice."

Fox didn't want to go, and Gus wouldn't make her. He told my mom that Fox had a favorite dress that she wanted to wear. But my mom insisted on taking me shopping. She made me try on dozens of dresses that she thought would be appropriate. I hated them all, but she finally bought me a red plaid jumper with a black turtleneck to wear underneath. "Not too dressy," she said. "But very cute."

On the evening of the ceremony, we drove to San

cousing

Francisco, which was about half an hour's drive from where we lived. My father was away on a business trip, so he couldn't be there. My mom had arranged to give Gus and Fox a ride.

I felt like an idiot in the red plaid jumper. Fox was wearing a dark-blue dress. Gus was wearing a gray suit. He said it was his "publisher suit" that he wore whenever he met with editors or publishers. But even in a suit, he still looked like Gus, and that helped a little.

Gus kept talking to Fox and me about how we'd be great, but I felt a little sick. Fox looked unhappy, too. It was so strange—the story had been ours and ours alone. Now that we had won, Mrs. Parsons thought it was hers and my mom thought it was hers and for all I knew the contest people thought it was theirs. Everyone thought they owned a piece of us. We were whittled away to nothing.

The ceremony was in a big old theater. Gus and my mom sat in the audience. Fox and I waited backstage with all the other girls who were reading their stories. Four high-school students were in one corner, pretending to talk about what books they had read but actually proving to each other how cool they were. The elementary-school kids were in another corner with a teacher—they were reading first. Fox and I were up in half an hour or so.

There was a young woman sitting by the door—a college student, I'd guess. As I watched, she pulled a makeup case from the pocket of her coat and put on lipstick. She looked, I thought, so cool and perfect. My mom wanted me to look like that, I thought, and there was no way I ever would.

We sat there for a minute, feeling uncomfortable and stupid. "Let's just leave," Fox said softly.

"What?"

"Let's just sneak out of here. This is no good. It isn't our story anymore."

I glanced at the door. "We can't do that."

"Sure we can." There was a note of pleading in her voice. "Who's going to stop us? We're the wild girls." She looked down at her hands. She wasn't Fox anymore. She was Sarah, and she was miserable. "It's all gone wrong."

I wasn't happy, either. The idea of getting up in front of all those people and reading our story made my stomach hurt.

"It's the clothes," I said. "How can we be wild girls, dressed like this? It just doesn't work."

"They don't want us to be wild," she said sadly. "Wild girls have dirt on their faces."

"Or war paint," I said. The fox girl had been wearing war paint when she met the princess.

As I watched, the college student stood up and walked down the hall to the ladies' room, leaving her coat draped over the back of the chair. I hesitated for a moment, and then stood up. "Come on," I said to Fox. She followed me over to the coat. I quickly dipped my hand into the pocket, grabbed the lipstick case, and kept walking until I found a spot backstage where no one would bother us.

The lipstick I had stolen was a lovely shade of deep red. Fox closed her eyes while I painted her forehead with wavy lines and spots, drew jagged lightning bolts on her cheeks and streaks on her chin. The lipstick felt cool and smooth on my face as Fox drew circles on my cheeks, lines on my forehead, a streak down my nose. I unbraided my hair—my mom had braided it tightly and neatly—and it frizzed around my face like a cloud.

"We're ready now," Fox said. She was grinning.

As the elementary-school girls were walking offstage, a woman was announcing our names. I grabbed Fox's hand and we walked to the microphone together. The woman at the podium stared at us, but I did not hesitate. I took the microphone from the woman's hand and stood still for a moment, staring out at the audience. Then I said the first line of the story, which I'd memorized months ago.

"We are the wild girls who live in the woods. You are afraid of us. You are afraid because you don't know what we might do."

That is the moment I remember. The hot lights on my face, the sweet, greasy scent of lipstick, the startled faces in the audience. The feeling of power and freedom as my voice rolled from the microphone, booming over the hall.

I looked out at the sea of faces—so many people, all watching us. I could see Gus—he was smiling. Beside him, my mom sat with her eyes wide and startled; Mrs.

Parsons was scowling. They were shocked. They were angry. They were afraid.

We were the wild girls who lived in the woods. We had won a contest, we had put on our war paint, and nothing would ever be the same again. We were the wild girls, and they did not know what we might do.

PART TWO
GOOD WITCH OR BAD?

7

A WAY OUT?

If this were just a story, it would end there. That was a moment of glory and triumph. But I'm not just writing a story—I'm telling you about my life. And life goes on. That's what Gus says, anyway.

While we were onstage, everything was wonderful. But we couldn't stay onstage forever. We walked offstage, listening to the audience applaud. Then we were backstage, and I looked at the lipstick on Fox's face and knew I had war paint on my face, too. I thought about seeing my mom staring up from the audience, and I felt a little dizzy.

"That was great!" Fox said. "Did you see the look on Mrs. Parsons's face?"

"Yeah." I was still thinking about the look on my mom's face. I was thinking about all the dresses my mom had made me try on when we went shopping. She had been looking for the one that was just right, the one that matched her image of what I should look like onstage. That image had not included war paint and frizzy hair.

"I've got to wash my face," I said. I knew that I was in a

world of trouble with no way back. "Come on." I grabbed Fox's hand and dragged her after me.

✹   ✹   ✹

The ladies' restroom was a pink-tiled cavern that smelled of soap and face powder. Along one long wall was a marble counter with great big sinks and neat stacks of paper towels. Attached to the wall were soap dispensers that dusted your hand with white powder soap when you pushed on a lever.

"I've got to get this stuff off my face," I told Fox. "My mom's going to kill me."

Fox had hoisted herself up to sit on the marble counter beside the sink. She watched, frowning, as I wiped at the lipstick on my nose with a paper towel. "She's going to kill you even if you wash your face. So why bother to wash it off?"

The lipstick smeared but remained on my nose. I wet the towel, got some powdered soap on it, and rubbed at my nose. The towel turned red, but there was still lipstick left on my nose.

I was imagining what my mom would say. *I don't know how you could do something like this.*

"You're just making it worse," Fox said.

It couldn't get any worse, I thought. Then I thought about my mom telling my father and my brother that I had painted my face, and I realized that it could all get much worse. I tried to cling to the feeling of power I had felt onstage, but that feeling was gone.

"We wrote a great story," Fox said.

"Yeah." I couldn't say any more, not to Fox. What I wanted to say was: *Yeah, it was a great story. But it was just a story. In the real world, the evil king wins. In the real world, you end up standing in the ladies' room with lipstick on your face, knowing that you're in trouble. In the real world, no good witch comes to show you the way through the enchanted forest.* I felt like crying.

"I've got to get this stuff off my face," I said again.

The door to the ladies' room opened, and I looked in that direction, expecting to see my mom or Mrs. Parsons bearing down on me.

A woman stepped in. I guessed she was in her late twenties. She wore a short black dress, black boots, and a sweater covered with black sequins. She smiled when she saw us. She wore big silver hoop earrings. Her short blonde hair stuck out in all directions—but it looked like she wanted it that way.

"Ah, it's the wild girls. Everybody's looking for you."

I stared at her, caught in a moment of panic.

"You won for best presentation," she said. "They wanted you to come up and get the trophy, but no one knew where you'd gone. Your English teacher went up and got it for you. She seemed a little flustered, but she thanked the judges very nicely."

"I guess she was surprised," Fox said.

"I think so," the woman said. "She didn't seem like the sort of teacher to advise students to wear war paint onstage."

"She's not," Fox said.

It was strange. Usually Fox didn't do much talking around strangers. Then I realized that the war paint made her brave.

The woman's smile widened. She went on. "I'm so glad I found you two. I wanted to tell you how much I liked the story. And your presentation was marvelous."

I stared at her, not knowing what to say.

"Newt wants to get this stuff off her face," Fox said. She gazed at the woman steadily. "We didn't plan for this part."

"Did you plan for the rest of it?"

"Not really," Fox said. "We were just going to read the story. But Newt's mom made us get dressed up, and that just wasn't right. So Newt stole this lipstick and . . ." Fox shrugged.

I shot Fox a panicky look. What was she thinking, talking about how I had stolen the lipstick? I was already in enough trouble.

The woman had crossed the room and set her purse on the counter beside the heap of lipstick-smeared paper towels. She nodded, looking at my dress. "Yeah, the dress doesn't really match the story. But the war paint made it work. Very effective contrast."

She snapped open her purse and took out a small bottle of lotion. "Here, try this. Smear it on your face and wipe it off with a paper towel."

The lipstick came off smoothly, leaving my cheek clean.

"Use the whole bottle," the woman said. "It was a free sample. I figure it couldn't go to a better cause."

"Thanks." My throat was tight, but I managed to get the word out.

"Her mom is going to be pissed," Fox was saying.

"So didn't your mother like the story, Newt?" the woman asked.

"My name is Joan," I said, correcting her. "Fox is the only one who calls me Newt. And *her* name is Sarah."

"Joan and Sarah," the woman repeated. "Nice to meet you, whatever you choose to call yourselves. My name's Verla Volante."

I stopped wiping my face and turned to look at her.

"What kind of name is Verla Volante?" Fox asked. *Rude*

Verla smiled. "It's a name I made up." She was still watching me. "So tell me—did your mother like the story?"

I thought about that. "I don't know," I said. "She read it, but she didn't say much about it."

"Ah," Verla said. "I think it would be a difficult story for a mother to comment on."

"She was happy that it won a prize."

"That's a start," Verla said.

I returned to cleaning my face. "But she's not going to be happy that I wore war paint when I read it. She kept saying that she wanted us to look nice."

"Are you happy you wore war paint?" Verla asked.

I hesitated, remembering the moment when I looked out at the audience. I glanced at Fox, who was grinning again. "Yeah, I guess I am."

"In the end, that's what matters," Verla said. "It's your story, after all."

"That's right," Fox said.

I wiped away the last of the lipstick. My face was a little pink from the rubbing, but that was all. I handed Fox the bottle of lotion and studied Verla. She acted like wearing war paint to read a story to a couple of hundred people was an everyday sort of thing. Like it was normal.

"You know, I'm running a summer writing class for talented kids," Verla said. "I think the two of you should apply to the program. You'd really like it, I think."

"You're a teacher?" I stared at her. She sure didn't look like a teacher. Too young, for one thing. For another, she thought war paint was a good idea. That didn't seem like something a teacher would think.

"I'm a writer, mostly," Verla said. "But sometimes I teach writing. That's what I'm doing this summer. This class lasts for eight weeks. You come to class once a week for seven weeks. Then, in the eighth week, you do a public reading like the one you just did. I already know you'll be great at that."

Fox was looking in the mirror and wiping lotion from her face with a paper towel. Nice that Verla thought we'd like her writing class, but I wasn't so sure. I remembered the moment just before we put on our war paint. Wouldn't a writing class be more of the same? We'd write stuff, but it wouldn't belong to us. People like Mrs. Parsons would be bugging us about our metaphors, and everyone would think our stories belonged to them.

"The class is offered through the University of California at Berkeley," Verla said. "It's very prestigious. Very important. Do you think your mother would like that?"

I nodded slowly. "Yeah. She probably would."

"Suppose I told your mother that I was very impressed by your performance, especially by the war paint. Suppose I mentioned that this is a very exclusive program, but I wanted to invite you both to attend." She glanced at Fox. "How do you think she'd react?"

"She'd be very happy," I said.

"Shall I go talk to her?" she asked, still watching my face.

I hesitated. She wasn't offering me a way back, but she was offering me a way out. "Just once a week for eight weeks," she said.

"Okay," I said. "Talk to my mom."

You know, maybe I was wrong about the good witch.

★　★　★

When we went back out to the lobby with our newly scrubbed faces, we found Verla Volante talking with my mom, Gus, and Mrs. Parsons.

"This is Miss Volante from the University of California," my mom told me. "She liked your story and your dramatic presentation. She said she liked the war paint, and I told her that I was surprised by it." She gave me a look that I couldn't quite figure out.

I nodded but didn't say anything.

My mom rested a hand on my shoulder. "We were talking about a summer program that she thinks you might like," my mom said. "I think it sounds like a wonderful opportunity."

And so Fox and I signed up for Verla Volante's summer writing class.

*   *   *

When I was in elementary school, I was really into fairy tales. I had an old copy of a Grimm Brothers' collection that my mom bought at a yard sale. And I found a collection of Hans Christian Andersen's fairy tales in the library and read it from cover to cover three times. I also really liked the *Wizard of Oz* movie.

So I knew about witches. There were good witches, like Glinda in *The Wizard of Oz*. And there were bad witches, like the Wicked Witch of the West. Then there were witches like the sea witch in Hans Christian Andersen's story "The Little Mermaid."

In that story, the little mermaid fell in love with a prince. She wanted to know how she could win the love of the prince, so she went to talk to the sea witch. The witch lived in a house built of bleached human bones. She kept fat water snakes as pets. It was a terrible place.

The little mermaid didn't need to tell the sea witch

why she had come; the witch already knew. That was one thing about witches—they knew what was going on, usually before you knew yourself. The witch knew what the little mermaid wanted. She also knew that it was a silly thing to want. She told the little mermaid as much: *I can get rid of your fish tail and send you up on land with legs, but that won't make you happy. In fact, it will make you miserable; every step you take will be agonizing. But if that's what you want, I can fix it. You just have to give me your voice.*

It wasn't a good deal. The little mermaid *was* miserable. But I couldn't really fault the witch. She explained the deal to the little mermaid, and the idiot went for it. I suppose she figured she didn't have a choice. She was in love with the prince, and she had to go for it.

That brought me to Verla Volante. I had no doubt that she was a witch. Oh, I didn't think she cooked up potions and worked spells, though I wouldn't have put that past her. But she knew too much. And I made a deal with her. She offered me a way out of trouble, and I took it.

I'd made a deal like the little mermaid, and it was too late to change my mind. We were going to Verla's class, and Verla Volante was a witch. The only question I had was this: Was she a good witch or a bad witch?

* * *

The day after the reading, Fox and I had our picture in the arts section of the local newspaper. Apparently a reporter had been in the audience. He wrote about our story and our presentation, calling it "the highlight of the evening."

Gus complimented us on our good review, and Fox thought we looked great. I wasn't so sure about that. Mrs. Parsons posted the article on the bulletin board outside her classroom but didn't include the photo. I figured she didn't want to give people ideas.

That was the last week of school. The next Saturday afternoon, the Girl Scouts had a pool party at Cindy's house. About a dozen girls came over, and we had an awards ceremony. Cindy's mom presented the pins and patches that we had earned over the school year. A couple of girls got patches for selling lots of cookies or doing various projects. Colleen had corresponded with a Girl Scout who lived in India. Sue had started making jewelry and had sold it at a craft fair. People talked about their projects. Then we swam and hung out by the pool.

It wasn't a bad group. We were not, to be sure, the cool kids in our school. The girls who aspired to be cool were practicing their cheerleading skills, learning to put on makeup in the bathroom, and talking incessantly about which boys were cute. They weren't selling cookies or doing projects. The Girl Scout troop gave uncool girls like us a group to hang out with.

The party broke up slowly—moms stopped by to pick the other girls up. Eventually, Cindy and I were the only ones left sitting by the pool. That was when Cindy mentioned the story in the newspaper.

"I saw your picture in the paper," she said. "Congratulations on winning 'Best Presentation.'"

"Thanks." The story Cindy had written for the contest hadn't made it into the winning group.

"I liked your story a lot better than the stuff you wrote for Mrs. Parsons's class," she said.

"What? You read it?" I pulled the beach towel tighter around my shoulders, trying to act normal about it but feeling uncomfortable.

"Yeah. Your mom gave my mom a copy."

"I didn't know my mom was showing the story around."

"I thought it was a really good story," Cindy said. She was trying to make me feel better, I think. "I liked the way it ended. When I was halfway through, I was thinking that maybe some handsome prince was going to show up and save the princess."

"She didn't need a handsome prince," I said. "Those wild girls did just fine on their own."

Cindy nodded. "I'm glad it worked out that way. I figured she wasn't one of the glamour patrol."

Sue had come up with that name for the girls who painted their fingernails and wore eye makeup and earrings and the shortest skirts they could get away with.

I laughed. "I couldn't even think like a member of the glamour patrol!" I said.

"What are you going to write next?" Cindy asked.

Fox and I hadn't finished another story yet. "I don't know. But I guess I'll find out." I told her about Verla Volante and about how she had appeared out of nowhere to rescue us. I told Cindy about the summer writing class.

"Verla Volante? Is that really her name?" Cindy asked.

I shrugged. "That's what she says her name is. She says she's a writer. I looked in the library for her books, but I couldn't find any."

"A writer? That's really cool," Cindy said.

I smiled. Cindy was all right. Most kids would have made a face and said something about not wanting to go to summer school, but Cindy sounded really excited. She was going to Hawaii on vacation with her family, but she actually sounded like she'd rather be in Verla's class.

SISTERS OF THE CRYSTAL TEARDROP

Fox and I started working on a story in which the wild girls traveled through the enchanted forest to the cave of a witch, who looked a lot like Verla Volante. The wild girls didn't know if she was a good witch or a bad witch. An enchanted fox was their guide.

When Fox and I went to our first class with Verla, we took BART from the suburbs where we lived to the University of California at Berkeley. BART stands for Bay Area Rapid Transit, the commuter trains that run from the suburbs into Oakland, Berkeley, and San Francisco. We didn't really want any guides, but we had two: Gus and my mom.

Gus had volunteered to take us both to Berkeley on BART. He said that he could do research for his next book in the university library while we were in class.

But my mom insisted on coming along to the first class. "We can all go together," she said. "While Gus does his research, I'll do some shopping."

The BART trains run in tunnels beneath Berkeley's

streets. The Berkeley BART station is underground. We stepped off the train onto a platform that was cool and shadowy, with redbrick walls and slick white floors. My mom led the way. Under one arm, she clutched her big brown purse as if someone might try to snatch it from her. In her other hand, she held a map of Berkeley.

An escalator carried us up from the shadowy station into the brilliant morning sunlight. I could hear music: a dance tune played on a violin.

No magic was involved—no wizards, no witches, no spell—but it felt like an enchanted place. In *The Wizard of Oz*, a tornado carries Dorothy to a magical land. In *The Lion, the Witch and the Wardrobe*, four children discover a door in the back of an old wardrobe and walk through it into the magical kingdom of Narnia.

Going up the escalator felt kind of like that. As it carried us up into the sunshine, I knew we were entering a different world where I didn't know the rules. The violin music was like a soundtrack to my own personal movie. I didn't know what would happen, but I knew it would be interesting. It would be dangerous. Like the wild girls in the woods, I didn't know what to expect.

The escalator came up in the center of a pavilion in a small plaza. The sky was blue, and the sun was shining. On the redbrick plaza that surrounded the pavilion, there was a sort of flea market: people were selling jewelry and T-shirts from card tables. College students—guys in

T-shirts and jeans, girls in tank tops and jeans or summer dresses and sandals—wandered among the tables.

On the street corner a guy with long brown hair tied back in a braid was playing a lively dance tune. He wore a T-shirt that said QUESTION AUTHORITY. A dog with a red bandana tied around its neck slept at his feet.

At the top of the escalator, a college girl in a sundress handed me a bright yellow flier—something about a special at a coffee shop.

"What's going on?" Fox asked the girl, waving a hand at the people in the plaza. "Some kind of festival?"

The girl laughed. "Just an ordinary day in Berkeley," she said.

I stepped away from the escalator and glanced at my mom, assuming she would be consulting her map, preparing to rush us off to class. But I was wrong about that. She was still clutching her purse and the map, but she was smiling, watching the guy with the violin.

"I know that song," she said. She sounded surprised and delighted.

I stared at her in shock. Maybe it was magic. She was tapping her foot in time to the music.

"What is it? Sounds like some kind of Russian dance tune," Gus said.

"Not Russian," my mom said. "It's a Polish polka. They always played it at weddings when I was a girl."

"Where did you grow up?" Gus asked.

"Alberta, Canada. Out in the country." She waved a hand, as if dismissing her childhood as unimportant, but she continued smiling.

"Campus is that way," Gus said. "We can walk, or we can wait for the bus to campus. But it's not a long walk."

"It's a beautiful day," my mom said. "Let's walk."

I stared at her, amazed. She sounded so cheerful and lighthearted.

She and Gus started out across the plaza. Gus continued asking questions about where she grew up. "Wheat-farming country," my mom said. "Mostly Polish and Ukrainian families. My father came over from the Ukraine."

Fox and I followed. I tried not to stare at the people around us, but it was difficult. We passed a man reading tarot cards for a young woman. We passed a woman with a parrot on her shoulder.

My mom stopped to look at a street vendor's table filled with jewelry that sparkled like precious gems. She lifted a ruby red pendant that was shaped like a teardrop, holding it up to the light. Streaks of gold ran through the ruby, like shafts of sunlight cutting through a crimson sunset sky. "Isn't that beautiful?" she asked me.

For once, my mom was right. All of the pendants were beautiful.

"They're made of fused glass," said the woman behind the table. "Every one is different."

"Look at this one," Fox said, touching a pendant that was deep amber with streaks of crimson and the faintest touch of blue. It was like the flickering light of a flame.

"And this one," I said, holding up an iridescent pendant. The sunlight shimmered on the glass—sometimes silver, sometimes blue. It reminded me of the moonlight on the fur of the fox I had seen in the orchard.

While the three of us examined the pendants, Gus stepped to one side. I looked up and saw him hand the woman some money.

"Choose your favorite," he said. "A pendant for each of you."

I chose the iridescent pendant. The woman threaded it on a leather thong and tied it around my neck so that it rested in the hollow of my throat. Fox chose the amber pendant.

My mom was about to walk away, when Gus said, "Hey, you didn't make your choice."

My mom frowned, confused.

"All the girls get pendants," he said. "To mark the special occasion."

My mom laughed, shaking her head. "Oh, you can't . . ." she began.

"Sure I can," Gus said. "It's important to mark new beginnings. Humor me."

My mom smiled and chose the crimson pendant.

"There you go," Gus said, smiling down at Fox. "The Sisters of the Crystal Teardrop."

I touched the pendant that rested in the hollow of my throat and noticed that Fox and my mom were both touching their pendants at the same time. I caught Fox's eye, and she grinned at me.

"I'm happy to be a member of the club," my mom said, and she was smiling, too.

We continued across the plaza, through the streets of Berkeley, and onto the university campus. My mom still carried her map, but she didn't bother to consult it. Gus knew the way, and we all followed him.

Gus was telling my mom about a job he once had working for a glass blower. He was talking about how amazing it was to watch glass change in the kiln from rock solid to a molten liquid, to watch sharp-edged shards of glass round and slump as they warmed up. "That pendant you're wearing was heated to at least fifteen hundred degrees to make the colors fuse. It's really been through the fire," he said.

It was strange to watch my mom with Gus. When she had met him for the first time, the sleeves of his Hawaiian shirt had covered his tattoo. She had looked startled when he showed up at BART wearing black jeans and a black tank top that showed off the tattoo. If you didn't know him, you might figure him for a biker, looking for trouble.

But she hadn't said anything about the tattoo. And as we walked across campus, she talked with him as if they were old friends.

The path led between big stone buildings. College students playing Frisbee on the grass were shouting to each other, large and careless.

I was wearing jeans and a red tank top. I had chosen the clothes carefully, walking a narrow line. My clothes had to be acceptable to my mom. But they also had to be something that I could feel good in.

I was wearing a bra. During the last year, my breasts had started to develop. My chest wasn't flat anymore. I wasn't really sure how I felt about that.

In our story, the princess had dressed like a boy when she was escaping into the enchanted forest. She had bound her breasts to squash them flat so no one would know she was a girl. I couldn't get away with that—my mom would have wanted to know what was going on.

So instead I had gone shopping with my mom to buy a bra. The ones we bought weren't much: scraps of stretchy material that cradled my growing breasts and contained them. I was wearing one of those bras now. It made me feel grown-up—but kind of strange. Like I had something to hide.

North Gate Hall, the building we were looking for, was not one of the big stone buildings, and I was glad of that. It was on the northern edge of campus. Its low walls were covered with wooden shingles, making it look more like a cabin in the woods than part of a college.

The room where our class met had windows that looked out on the redwood trees. Verla Volante was just inside the door, standing behind a table. She was wearing a blue denim skirt and a shirt with big red flowers on it. She still wore silver hoop earrings, and her blonde hair still stuck out in all directions.

"Hey, wild girls," she said. "Welcome. Come on in. Make yourself a name tag, and find a seat." She gestured to the markers and name tags on another table a little farther inside the room.

My mom started asking Verla questions; Gus stayed nearby, listening. Fox and I moved to the table with the name tags.

I chose a thick red marker and neatly printed JOAN on a name tag. I glanced over at Fox. She was holding a brown marker and frowning at a name tag.

"What's the matter?" I asked her softly.

"I don't know whether I should write 'Fox' or 'Sarah,'" she whispered back.

I looked down at my name tag. I didn't want to be Newt here. The newts in the stream were shy and careful, and that wasn't how I wanted to be here. Joan was the right choice for me. But what about Fox?

"This isn't school," I said. "That's where you're Sarah. Here you could be Fox, I think." I wanted her to be Fox—outspoken and confident.

"Hi." A guy with curly red-brown hair had just come up to the table. "So, should we use our own names or adopt aliases?"

He was wearing a faded T-shirt and jeans with fraying cuffs, but he wore them with complete confidence. A smart kid who knew he was smart and wasn't afraid who else knew it—his question told me that.

He grinned at us. "My friends call me Bodie, but my birth certificate says I'm Baldemar. My mom studied German folklore in college and took it out on me."

"What would you use as an alias?" I asked.

"That's the problem. I haven't figured that out yet. I guess I'll stick with Bodie."

"I'm Fox," Fox said. She had made a decision.

Bodie raised one eyebrow. "Really?"

"Absolutely," Gus said, coming up behind Fox. "It's not on her birth certificate, but it might as well be."

I saw Bodie's eyes widen just a bit as he took in Gus and his tattoo.

"I'm Gus, Fox's dad."

"Time to get started!" Verla Volante called from the other side of the room. "Parents and friends, say goodbye. Young writers, find a seat. We've got stories to write and not enough time to do it."

Fox and I found a seat at the side of the room toward the back, where we could look out the window at the redwoods. Bodie took a seat beside us. Gus and my mom waved as they left.

There were ten kids in the room. Five girls and five guys, all about my age or little older. Some were sitting attentively, looking at Verla. The good students, I thought. Bodie was talking to another guy. A girl with long blonde hair in the front row was talking with a dark-skinned girl. The blonde girl looked kind of like she might belong to her school's glamour patrol. I pegged her as someone who wouldn't want to have anything to do with me and Fox.

In that first class, Verla asked a lot of really strange questions. Not like most teachers, who ask a lot of questions that they know the answers to. Verla asked weird questions, and she said stuff like: *You're the only one who knows the answer to this question. Questions like these don't have right or wrong answers. If you don't know the answer, make up an answer. Later on you can figure out if it's true.*

Here are some questions she asked.

- *What was the first thing you heard when you woke up this morning?*
- *If you got to take one thing from your bedroom before a meteor hit your house and destroyed everything, what would you take?*
- *What does your room smell like?*
- *What would you most like to eat for breakfast? Why?*
- *How do you feel about papaya?* (That last one was a question for Jose, who wanted papaya for breakfast because that's what he had when he was visiting his grandmother in Mexico.)
- *What's your favorite color?* (Verla's favorite color was ultraviolet. She said that ultraviolet was an invisible color, just outside the range of colors people can see. But bees could see ultraviolet even though people couldn't.)

Verla was always moving around, pacing up and down

in front of the class. She wrote questions on the black-board—as if we needed more questions.

- *What scares you? Why are you afraid of that?*
- *If you had ten thousand dollars and you had to spend it all in the next hour, what would you buy?*

Once, when Jose was looking down at his paper, doodling, Verla threw an eraser at him. It smacked him on the head. After that, no one doodled. We all kept an eye on her.

"You've got to pay attention," she said. "When you write a story, you want the person reading to see and hear and smell the world you make up. Pay attention and describe what you see." She told us that some people say you should use words to paint a picture of the world. But Verla said that painting a picture isn't good enough. You need to open a door so that people can walk into your world. When they walk through that door, you want them to see the world, smell the world, and hear the sounds of the world. To do that, you have to pay attention to all those things yourself. You have to learn the truth about the world.

When she looked at me, I got the feeling that she could see what I was thinking. Her hair was wild, and her eyes were blue and intense. She looked more wide awake than anyone I'd ever met. She was paying attention, all right.

It was exciting. It was exhausting. You had to keep thinking, thinking, thinking. The writing was the least of my worries. She didn't care how you wrote down the answers. She just wanted you to think of the answers and write them down in your notebook.

The first thing I had heard in the morning was a mockingbird. This mockingbird liked to sit on our chimney and sing. The song echoed in the chimney. Sometimes the mockingbird sang the songs of other birds, but sometimes it imitated a ringing phone or a car horn. My father hated that mockingbird because it woke him up on Saturdays and Sundays, when he wanted to sleep late. He said he was going to shoot it with a BB gun. But no one could find Mark's old BB gun. That's because I found that BB gun and hid it in the back of my closet the first time my father said that he wanted to shoot the bird. I liked the mockingbird.

If a meteor were just about to hit the house, I'd grab my notebook and the quilt that my grandmother gave me when I was six years old. My gramma made that quilt. I didn't know I even cared about it, but it was the second thing I thought of.

My room didn't smell like anything that I could think of. I made a note to spend some time sniffing when I was in my room to see what it smelled like.

I wanted to eat pancakes for breakfast because my mom used to make pancakes for breakfast on Sundays when we lived in Connecticut. She hadn't done that since we moved, and I kind of wondered why.

"Okay," Verla said at last. "So far, I've been asking

questions and you've been answering them. Hearing people's answers to those questions has helped you get to know the people in this class. Right?"

We all nodded. I knew that Bodie woke to cello music, because his mom practiced the cello in the garden outside his window every morning, and that Ketura's room smelled like lavender, because her grandmother had given her lavender cologne for her birthday. I knew that Matthew would spend his ten thousand dollars on a new stereo and a bunch of records. I knew that Fox had eaten cold pizza for breakfast and that Verla had eaten peanut butter on toast and washed it down with chocolate milk.

"Now it's your turn," Verla said. "I want you to figure out what questions to ask someone so that you can get to know them better."

Verla had us pair up. She didn't let us choose our own partners, or I would have been with Fox. Instead, she pointed, saying, "You and you." Fox was paired with Ketura. I was paired with Priscilla, the blonde who looked like she was with the glamour patrol.

"You have five minutes," Verla said. "Find out something interesting to share with the class. You can take notes if you like."

"Do you want to ask the first question, or should I?" Priscilla asked.

"You can go first."

Pay attention, Verla had said. I watched as she opened her notebook and picked up her pen, as if she were going to write down every word I said. Up close, she didn't look so much like a member of the glamour patrol. She had long blonde hair, but she wasn't wearing lip gloss or eye shadow or anything like that. She wasn't wearing earrings, but she had a silver cross on a chain around her neck.

"What's your favorite animal?" she asked me.

I answered with the first thing that came to mind. "The mockingbird."

"Why?"

"Because it never sings the same song twice. It never gets boring," I said. "What's your favorite animal?"

"Gecko," she said.

"Really?" I knew a gecko was a kind of lizard, and I never figured that she'd have a lizard as her favorite animal.

"When we lived in Indonesia, I had a gecko that lived in my room. It ran around on the ceiling at night."

I looked at her with new respect. "What were you doing in Indonesia?"

"My dad was a missionary, so we lived there for a year."

I was going to ask more about Indonesia, but she asked another question. "What's your favorite book?"

I had just finished reading *The Hobbit* and now I was reading *The Lord of the Rings*. "*The Hobbit*, I guess."

"What's that about?"

"About this magic world where there are wizards and elves."

She was frowning. "My mom doesn't let me read books with magic in them."

"Really? Why?"

"She says she's not sure whether they're appropriate."

"Wow." I was starting to feel kind of sorry for her. She was pretty and all, but it sounded like her parents were really strict. "So what's your favorite book?"

"I should probably say the Bible." Then she smiled shyly. "My dad's a minister, and the Bible is the best book there is." Priscilla leaned a little closer. "But I also really like a book that my grandmother gave me. Hans Christian Andersen's fairy tales."

I nodded, smiling at her. "Hey, I've read those."

"Remember," Verla said. "You're not just chatting here. You want to find out what makes this person tick. Take a minute and think hard about two more questions. Don't be afraid to be nosy."

Two questions. I looked around the room, trying to think of questions that were clever and revealing.

"Time to ask," Verla said.

I looked at Priscilla and asked the first question that came into my head. "How come you're wearing that cross?"

She touched the silver cross. "My mom gave it to me to remind me of Jesus. How come you are wearing that pendant?"

"I came here with my friend Fox. Her dad bought us these pendants from a street vendor," I said. "He said we were Sisters of the Crystal Teardrop."

"One last question," Verla said.

I asked her, "If you were going to use an alias, what would it be?" It wasn't really my question. It was the question that Bodie had asked us before class. But it was a really good question, I thought.

"An alias?"

"Yeah. An alias or a nickname. What would it be?"

She bit her lip, thinking. "I never much liked being called Priscilla. It's such a old-fashioned name."

"What would you rather be called?"

"Um . . . my last name's Zumer. I think my alias would be Zoom." She smiled when she said it.

I nodded. "That's cool." Zoom was a great alias, I thought. Just thinking of Priscilla as Zoom made her seem like a different person.

✳ ✳ ✳

Verla had us pull our chairs into a circle, and she asked us what questions we had asked. People kept raising their hands and telling Verla their questions: *What's your favorite subject in school? What do you like to do after school? What do you want to do when you grow up? What's your favorite food? What do your parents do for a living? Do you have any pets?*

Verla liked all the questions. She was more enthusiastic than any teacher I'd ever had. She talked about how each question helped you understand a person better. She talked about describing people and making them seem like real people. "What a person is like inside may be very different from what they look like from the outside. When you write about people, you want to show what they are like inside—by showing what they like and what they don't like, by showing how they talk to other people, by talking about where they live, where they grew up."

In my notebook, I wrote down all the questions people asked and all the questions that Verla Volante mentioned.

"Okay, now it's time to introduce your partner. Let's start with Bodie and go clockwise around the circle. I know you probably have lots to say, but I want you to choose just one interesting thing about your partner."

"This is Al," Bodie said, waving a hand at the boy beside him. Al was earnest-looking, with dark hair and glasses. "He has a pet boa constrictor named Mr. Squeeze."

"This is Bodie," Al said. "He walks on stilts and juggles." He looked at Verla. "I guess that's two things."

We went around the circle and learned something about everyone. Jose liked basketball. Samantha was getting her braces off in a month. Tyler had been to London. Matthew could speak Russian because his mom was Russian. Ketura said that Fox's dad was a writer, and everyone looked impressed about that.

Then it was Priscilla's turn to say something about me. I figured she would say that my favorite animal was the mockingbird, but she didn't. "This is Joan," she said. "She belongs to the Sisterhood of the Crystal Teardrop." When she said it like that, it sounded really important.

Then everyone was looking at me, and I had to say something about Priscilla.

"This is Priscilla," I said. "But when I asked her what her alias would be, she said it was 'Zoom.' And I think she seems more like a Zoom than a Priscilla."

"I think you're right," Verla said. "And that was a very good question."

"It wasn't really my question. Bodie asked that when we were doing name tags."

Bodie grinned.

Verla nodded. "Nice of you to share the credit," she said. "It was still a fine question to ask."

✱　✱　✱

At noon, we got to take a break and go eat lunch. By that time, I needed a rest.

Fox and I sat on a low stone wall right near North Gate Hall. Most of the other kids were going to the deli across the street to buy lunch, but my mom had packed sandwiches for us. I thought about going with the rest of the kids to get a drink, but I felt a little shy about that. Everyone in the class seemed so smart and together. It was good just to sit with Fox.

"So do you think she's a good witch or a bad witch?" Fox asked.

We had spent most of the previous afternoon talking about Verla Volante. "I don't think she's a bad witch," I said. "Maybe she's neither good nor bad?"

"That's probably about right," Fox said.

"Isn't that true of everybody?" Bodie had come up, carrying his sandwich from the deli.

I stared at him, wondering how much he had over-heard. Talking about Verla as a witch probably sounded pretty goofy. "What's that?" I asked.

"Most people are neither good nor bad, but some of each, I think."

"I suppose so," I said.

"Do you mind if I join you?" Bodie asked. He didn't wait for an answer. He sat on the wall beside me. "What do you think of the class so far?" he asked.

"It's interesting," I said cautiously. I glanced at Fox. She was watching Bodie with suspicion.

"My dad's a professor here," he said. "He knows Verla by reputation."

He used her first name easily, as if they were equals. Thinking about it, I realized he had reacted to Gus in the same way. This kid had an air of unshakable confidence.

"Yeah? So what's her reputation?"

"Brilliant but eccentric," he said. "Noted as a poet, essayist, short story writer, and teacher. Unconventional. She usually teaches university students, and they either love her or hate her."

"I can see that." I already knew which I'd be. Even if she was a bad witch, she was one of the most interesting people I'd ever met.

"What do you think of the other students?" he asked.

I shrugged, not willing to commit to an opinion. "I don't really know them yet."

"Well, here's my take: we're a bunch of loose nuts." He

laughed when he saw my expression. "I mean that in the nicest possible way, of course." He leaned forward. "So tell me: are you in with the in-crowd in your school? Do you hang out with the cheerleaders and the jocks?"

I laughed. Fox was looking at him as if he had gone crazy.

"I figured. And you probably don't hang out with the smart kids. You know, the hard-core nose-to-the-grind-stone crowd."

I shook my head.

"And I don't think you're one of the dopers or losers."

"Well, thanks for that," I said.

"Loose nuts," he repeated, grinning. "Verla has gathered all the loose nuts from a bunch of different schools. These are the kids who belong to the chess club; the ones who build scenery for the school play or put out the school newspaper; the ones who hide in the background, staying out of the way of the popular kids. Some of them are art kids, some of them are just loose nuts."

"What do you mean? Art kids."

"You know—they're smart kids, but they aren't in with the in-crowd. They are more or less a bunch of outcasts who hang out with other outcasts. You know what I mean?"

I stared at him. I hadn't thought of it that way, but he was probably right. I glanced at Fox. She nodded. "Yeah," I admitted. "That fits."

"And since we got into this cool program, now we're the cool kids, right?" Bodie said.

I nodded, remembering how Cindy had acted when I told her about the class with Verla. "I guess so."

"And what makes it even better is we don't have to figure out who's smart. I figure everyone here is. From what I hear, Verla handpicked everyone."

"Hey, Bodie." It was Al, the boy with the boa constrictor.

"Hey, Al. How's it going?" Bodie turned back to us. "Al is one of the loose nuts from my school. You're in the chess club, aren't you, Al?"

"You bet," Al said. He didn't seem bothered by being labeled a loose nut. "All the best people are in the chess club."

"I'm not," Bodie said.

Al grinned. "See—there you go."

"Do you really have a boa constrictor?" Fox asked him.

"Yeah. I've had Mr. Squeeze since I was eight. Are you scared of snakes?"

Fox shook her head. "Nope. I catch garter snakes in the grass sometimes."

We sat in the sunshine and talked about snakes and ate lunch. Priscilla—who had changed her name tag to Zoom—joined us. I felt like we were in a new world—far from our school, where we were the ones who didn't fit.

We were surrounded by people who didn't fit. And here, we all fit just fine.

✳ ✳ ✳

After lunch, Verla talked about characters and asked more questions. I was starting to get a feel for the other kids in the class. Bodie was always the first one with his hand up: he liked to talk and he thought he knew everything. That could be annoying, but he actually did seem to know a lot, so that made it better. He wasn't the only smart one: everyone seemed pretty sharp. Ketura and Samantha didn't raise their hands much, but they always had something to say when Verla called on them.

At the end of class, she gave us two homework assignments. "It's going to be a week before we meet again," she said. "So you have time to do both assignments."

"First, I want you to interview someone who is at least fifteen years older than you are. Find out where that person was when he or she was your age. What were they doing? What did they care about? What were their plans, their hopes, their dreams? Write down your questions and their answers. That's the first assignment.

"Second, I want you to write about something that really scares you. Any questions?"

There were many questions. How long should the interview be? What kinds of questions should we ask? Where were we supposed to find someone to interview?

"I'd guess most of you have some old folks living

in your house." Verla's tone was dry and a bit sarcastic. "Maybe you call them Mom or Dad. And I'd guess those folks are at least fifteen years older than you are."

I heard a woman laugh, and I turned to look. My mom and Gus were waiting in the back of the classroom with three other mothers. They were all grinning.

"That's it, then," Verla said. "Go off and have a good time. Come back with knowledge. Or at least a few good questions."

This book
reminds me of
to Kill a mockking
bird!

9

PICTURES OF PIGS

"I was wondering," I said when I got to Fox's the next morning, "do you suppose I could interview your dad?" I'd been thinking about it since class. I didn't want to interview my mom—that would be too boring. And there was no way I could interview my dad.

Fox was up in the old walnut tree. Sitting in the classroom for hours had left her with pent-up energy. We'd talked about building a tree house, and she had decided to get started. She'd scavenged half a dozen boards from a pile of lumber scraps by her house. Before I got there, she had managed to wedge two of them between two branches. Now she was sitting on one of the boards, looking down at me.

"Sure!" she said. "Can I interview your mom?"

I blinked at her, startled. She sounded really excited about it. "That's okay with me," I said. "If it's okay with you."

"Sure." Fox swung down from the tree. "Your mom

was really nice yesterday. I think interviewing her would be fun."

So we talked to Gus, and he said it was okay with him, and I called my mom. She said fine and why didn't we come home for lunch and then Fox could interview her.

We went to my house and had grilled-cheese sandwiches for lunch. Lunch with Fox usually meant peanut butter on crackers. I liked that fine, but I had to admit that it was great to have my mom's grilled-cheese.

After lunch, we went out on the patio and sat in lawn chairs.

My mom had spent the morning working in the backyard. She was wearing shorts and an old cotton shirt, and her hair was tied back in a ponytail. The pendant that Gus had bought her the day before hung around her neck. She looked more relaxed than I'd seen her in a while. This spring, she had planted a vegetable garden. Now she was putting in some flowerbeds.

"I'm ready to be interviewed," she said. "What do I do?"

"You just answer questions," I said. I looked at Fox. She was looking down at her notebook. Now that we were actually sitting with my mom, she was getting shy. "Fox is going to ask the questions, since it's her interview."

"Okay," my mom said.

Fox uncapped her pen, ready to write, and looked up from her notebook. "When you were my age, what was your favorite thing to do?" she asked.

Fox and I had spent the morning thinking of questions. That was one of them.

My mom frowned. "Just one thing? Or can I have two?"

It was funny to have my mom asking Fox's permission for anything. I think she did it to get Fox to relax. Fox looked surprised.

"It's your interview," my mom said. "You make the rules."

Fox smiled then. "Sure, you can have two," Fox said.

"When I was thirteen, I liked growing flowers and vegetables in the garden, and I liked painting pictures. That year, I won two prizes at the county fair. One for growing the perfect pumpkin and one for my watercolor painting of the sunflowers in the garden."

"The perfect pumpkin?" Fox said. "How was it perfect?"

I remembered seeing a photo on the wall in my gramma's living room. It showed my mom when she was a kid, standing beside a big pumpkin and grinning. I had never known the story behind that photo.

My mom shrugged. She was smiling. "I had been trying to grow the biggest pumpkin, but somebody else beat me on that. But the pumpkin that won for being biggest was all lopsided and gnarly. My pumpkin was really big— and it was beautiful. Symmetrical, round, just right for carving a jack-o'-lantern. I think the judges made up the 'perfect pumpkin' prize just because they wanted to give something to that pumpkin."

She laughed then. "I was really happy to win. Then my brothers called me 'Pumpkinhead' for the rest of the summer. I wasn't so happy about that."

Fox laughed. "Really?" she asked.

"Really. All summer long."

I stared at my mom, trying to imagine anyone calling her Pumpkinhead. It was hard to do.

"What about the sunflower picture? Was it the perfect sunflower picture?" Fox asked.

My mom shook her head. "No, there I just got an honorable mention. But I got a ribbon, and my picture hung in the art show along with all these pictures painted by grown-ups. There was a big ceremony, and I had to go up onstage to get my ribbon." She made a face then. "I didn't know there was going to be a ceremony. I was still in my grimy jeans from wrestling the pumpkin out of the truck, and I had to walk onstage like that. All of the other people on stage were grown-ups. All these women in nice dresses and me in my jeans." She shook her head. "That part wasn't so great. I felt like a dope."

I would have asked more about that, but Fox was the one doing the interviewing. I was just listening.

"What kind of pictures did you paint?"

"Back then, I painted with watercolors. I learned to paint with oils when I was in college, but that was messy and expensive and smelled bad. I liked watercolors better. Mostly I painted pictures of the farm—my mom's garden, the old barn, the pigs in their pen." She laughed. "Those pigs were great subjects. They slept all day, so it was easy to paint them. I liked my pig pictures better than those sunflowers, but the judges liked the sunflowers."

I stared at my mom, trying to imagine her standing by a pigpen, painting pictures of the pigs. There was a painting of pigs hanging in Gramma's living room, too. I wondered if that was my mom's.

"I thought I'd go on and paint lots of pictures and become famous," my mom said, still smiling. "But when I went to art school, I found out you couldn't make a living painting pictures of pigs, no matter how good they were. So I went into fashion illustration." She made a face. "I'd rather paint pictures of pigs."

Fox grinned. She was relaxed now. "Is that why you don't paint pictures anymore?"

"I suppose that's part of it. I met Joan's dad and we had Mark, and I didn't really have time anymore." She frowned, and then shrugged her shoulders. "Being a mom is more important than painting pictures." She looked at the flowerbed she'd dug up that morning. "I still like growing flowers and vegetables, though."

Fox asked her some questions about what she was going to plant in the garden, but I wasn't really listening. I was thinking about my mom up onstage in her grimy jeans beside all the ladies in their nice dresses. No wonder she had wanted us to dress up when our story won that prize. I kept thinking about how my mom had smiled when she talked about painting pictures of pigs. It was too bad she didn't paint pictures of pigs anymore.

* * *

That afternoon, I interviewed Gus. Fox brought him out to the clearing in the woods, and he sat in the easy chair. Fox perched in the tree, and I sat on the ground, leaning back against the tree with my notebook in my lap.

I asked him some of the questions that we had come up with in class. His favorite food was something called *pad thai.* (I didn't know what that was, and he said it was a Thai noodle dish, and we'd have to get some next time we were in Berkeley.) If a meteor were just about to hit the house, he'd take Fox. When Fox said he didn't have to take her because she'd take herself, he said he'd take the manuscript for the story he was working on right then. If he had ten thousand dollars and he had to spend it in an hour, he said he'd buy a gift certificate at the local bookstore. Then he could take his time figuring out what books he wanted to buy. I thought that was pretty smart.

"When you were our age, did you know you were going to be a writer?" I asked.

He shook his head.

"What did you think you were going to be?" I asked.

"I wanted to play in a band," he said. "I had an old guitar, and I started a band with a bunch of my friends."

"How come you became a writer instead?"

He leaned back in the easy chair, looking up at the

leaves of the walnut trees. "I read books when I was a kid, lots of books. Books always seemed like magic to me. They took you to the most amazing places. When I got older, I realized that I couldn't find books that took me to all of the places I wanted to go." He smiled. "To go to those places, I had to write some books myself."

*   *   *

When I got home that afternoon, my mom was weeding the vegetable garden. The air was cooling off, but it was still balmy. From someone else's yard, I heard the hum of a lawn mower. Our own yard could have used mowing. That was Mark's job. I knew that my father would get on his case about it soon.

My mom was pulling weeds that had sprouted between the tomato plants, and the air smelled of warm tomatoes. The plants were loaded with green tomatoes. A few were starting to redden.

I stood in the yard for a moment, watching her weed and realizing that she was always busy. *Pay attention,* Verla had said. *Notice things and think about what you notice.*

My mom was always working on one project or another. Making new cushions for the family-room sofa with trim carefully chosen to match the red flecks in the rug. Refinishing a rocking chair that she bought at a yard sale. Running a paper drive for the Girl Scout troop. Weeding a vegetable garden.

Sometimes, she tried to get me to help with these projects, and sometimes I did. I had spent an afternoon digging compost into the garden soil. I had helped her plant the beans. But usually I tried to dodge the projects. I counted myself as lucky when I managed to do that successfully.

"Have you come to help me weed?" my mom asked, looking up from her task.

"I guess I could," I said.

I went and put my notebook in my room, then came back to help. I started working just a few feet from where she was working. I was still thinking about the questions that Fox had asked her. Sitting there, I realized that my mom and I didn't really talk most of the time. Not like Fox had talked to her.

My mom asked me questions about what I was doing. She made suggestions that I didn't want to hear—like telling me I should be a Girl Scout or asking me why I wasn't taking a sweater. I complained when she bugged me. But we didn't really talk.

"I remember seeing a photo in Gramma's living room. You were standing by a pumpkin," I said. "Was that your perfect pumpkin?"

"It sure was. Gramma was as proud of that pumpkin as I was."

When I was eight, my father had gone on a business trip and my mom had taken my brother and me to Gramma's farm. We had driven all the way from Connecticut to Alberta, a long car trip. We drove on highways, on county roads, then on endless dirt roads.

My grandfather had died when I was six. My grandmother lived alone after that. Her sons, my uncles, farmed her land.

Gramma's house was surrounded by enormous flat fields of wheat. A few tall trees grew right by the small white house, casting a welcome shade. The barn had a hayloft where a mama cat lived with her kittens. The cats were wild: try as I might, I couldn't get them to come to me and be petted.

I remember Gramma milking the cow. From the cow's teat, Gramma squeezed a stream of milk, sending it up over the head of the mama cat. The cat leaped in the air after the milk, getting as much on her fur as in her mouth. But that didn't matter. She licked it off afterward.

I had already done my interview—I had interviewed Gus. But I still felt like asking questions. I thought about the questions that Fox and I had come up with that afternoon. "What scared you, when you were a kid?" I asked her.

"What scared me?" She stopped weeding for a moment and frowned at me.

"What was the scariest thing that ever happened to you?"

She thought for a moment. "Probably the thunderstorm," she said slowly.

"What thunderstorm?"

"I was caught in a thunderstorm, down by the creek." She sat back on her heels and continued. "We went there to fish, sometimes. Or to go for a swim on hot days. It was about a mile from home. I was fishing one day, not paying much attention, and I smelled a thunderstorm coming."

"What does a thunderstorm smell like?"

"The air gets cool and smells like rain. And I looked up and saw great dark clouds rising up. They'd been building for some time, but I hadn't been paying attention. Then I saw a flash of lightning and heard the thunder rumble. I ran for home, but the storm caught me. Thunder crashing all around and great flashes of light and I was running and running and the rain hammered down on me. I was drenched by the time I got home." She was smiling.

"It was scary?"

"Yeah, it was."

"But you're smiling."

"It was scary. The thunder was so loud and the lightning so bright. That storm was so powerful. But running through it, I got the feeling that I was powerful, too. Like I could do anything. I didn't even mind getting wet."

I stared at her, amazed. I tried to imagine her as a girl my age, running through a thunderstorm.

"I told my mother I had been in the barn. She would have been mad if she'd known I'd run all the way from the creek in the storm." My mom laughed. "My brother Ed knew. He saw me from the porch as I came running down the road. I had to give him my dessert at dinner that night so he wouldn't tell."

Uncle Ed was a tall, thin man with graying hair and

one bad knee. He walked with a cane. I tried to imagine him demanding my mom's cake. Power

My mom was still smiling. "Your turn now," she said. "What's the scariest thing you've ever done?"

I sat back on my heels. *Tell the truth,* Verla said. *To be a writer, you have to learn to tell the truth.*

I spoke quickly, before I could chicken out. "Painting my face with lipstick and going out to read that story." After the words were out of my mouth, I couldn't believe I had actually said them.

My mom stopped smiling. She studied my face. "If that was so scary, why did you do it?"

I looked down at my hands. I didn't know what to say. "I had to do something," I said at last. "It felt like everyone was taking our story away from us." I looked up. She was watching me, sitting very still.

"People were taking it away?" she said. "How were they taking it away?"

"Mrs. Parsons was acting like it was all her doing. And you . . ." I stopped, unable to keep going.

"I was very proud of you," she said. "You know that, don't you? I wanted you to go up there and look great and do great."

I nodded. "But Fox and I . . . we wrote a story about being different from everyone else. But . . . but then you wanted me to dress up so that I was just like everyone else."

My mom didn't say anything.

"And Fox . . . I mean Sarah, was so miserable about

the whole thing. I would have probably just toughed it out—stood up there and read the story no matter what. But Sarah was ready to run out the back door."

My mom nodded slowly. "She's not as tough as you are."

I blinked, startled by that.

"Anyway, I had to do something," I said. "So I got some lipstick, and I made us into wild girls. We were up onstage and everyone was clapping and it was great. But then we had to leave the stage."

"Then you knew you were in trouble."

I nodded. "Just like you knew you'd be in trouble if Gramma knew you'd been running through the thunderstorm."

My mom shook her head sadly. "When I imagined your reading, I thought you would look so pretty and dignified. And instead . . ." She stopped in the middle of the sentence.

"Instead, we looked like wild girls."

"I guess so. I had never imagined you as a wild girl. And there you were, covered in war paint." She shook her head again. "You didn't seem like my daughter, up there in your war paint. I'd never seen you do anything like that before."

I thought about the moment onstage when we read our story. "Maybe it was like being in the thunderstorm. When we were up there, I was powerful; I could do anything. Like you in the thunderstorm. And then I was in trouble."

My mother nodded. "Yeah. But I . . . I was okay with it, after a while."

"After Verla Volante talked to you," I said.

"That helped," she admitted. "Verla thought you were great."

"It was lucky that Verla Volante showed up," I said. "And I didn't even have to give her my dessert."

10

SOMETHING KIND OF SCARY

Talking to my mom was good, even though it felt kind of strange. I mean, it wasn't as though we were suddenly best friends, or anything like that. But I realized that I used to get along with my mom, back when we lived in Connecticut. I started fighting with her after my dad told us we were going to move. I was really mad about that, and maybe she was, too.

I spent the next day over at Fox's. "I like your mom," Fox told me. "The way you talked about her before, I thought she must be mean. But I think she's okay."

I had to agree.

That evening, my mom and dad went out after dinner. My mom said they had "an appointment."

The way my mom said "an appointment," I knew it wasn't a good idea to ask questions about where they were going. Verla might have thought questions were always good, but around my house, asking questions could get you in trouble. Asking my mom a bunch of questions about her childhood was okay, but I knew that asking a bunch of questions about this mysterious appointment would not be. So I kept my mouth shut.

After my parents left, Mark went over to Andrew's house to hang out and read comics. That was fine with me.

I copied over the interview with Gus, neatly writing my questions and his answers. Then I started thinking about the next assignment. We were supposed to write about something really scary. *Think carefully before you start writing,* Verla had said. *Think of lots of scary things before you choose one. You could choose something that most people are scared of—like walking on a tightrope high off the ground or crawling through a pit of poisonous snakes. That's okay, but it's not as interesting as writing about something that most people wouldn't find scary.*

I took my notebook and sat at the kitchen table. The sun had just gone down. The sky was a deep, rich blue. I had told Verla that blue was my favorite color, and she had told me to be more specific. *What shade of blue?* she had asked. The color of the sky at twilight was exactly my favorite color.

It wasn't day anymore, but it wasn't quite night. The world was changing from one to the other. There was a sense of peace: out there, birds were settling on their perches for the night. And there was a sense of anticipation: through the window, I watched a neighborhood cat stroll across the backyard, heading out to hunt. From the flowerbeds, crickets called to each other. Down at the creek, I knew frogs were doing the same, calling out in the darkness to let the other frogs know where they were.

Owls—like the one that scared me with its hooting when I went to Fox's that night—were waking up.

The kitchen was getting dark, but I didn't bother to turn on the lights. I liked it the way it was: dim and quiet, except for the calling crickets.

I thought about scary things. Spiders and ghosts and zombies. Most people were afraid of those things. I thought about walking through the orchard in the dark and about walking through the culvert with Fox. Those things had scared me at the time, but they didn't seem scary right now. Putting on war paint and reading with Fox had been terrifying, but now that I'd talked about it with my mom, it didn't seem so bad.

I heard the rattle of a key in the front door. Before I could get up, I heard the door open. My father's voice drowned out the sound of the crickets. ". . . a waste of time and money as far as I'm concerned," he was saying. "That counselor was an idiot."

My mom said something, but I couldn't make out the words, just the sound of her voice.

My father laughed—a harsh, unfriendly sound. "Of course you didn't think he was an idiot. He agreed with you. He didn't think I could do anything right."

My mom spoke again, a little louder now. "I'm sorry you got that impression. I thought—"

"I know what you thought. You thought I'd agree to keep spending money on this. Well, you're wrong about that."

"I thought it was helpful to have someone else's point of view," my mom said. Her voice was strained, apologetic. "I thought he might help us understand each other better."

"Oh, I understand a lot of things," my father said. "I understand that it cost me an arm and a leg to spend an hour talking with some quack about stuff we already know. I understand that you're spending money like it was water. You didn't tell me how much that fancy summer writing class for Joan was going to cost me. Waste of money, I'd say."

"That class is important for Joan," my mom said, her voice a little louder.

"I understand that those braces for Mark aren't going to be cheap, either. I understand that I had to waste an evening talking to an idiot." My father's voice, already loud, was getting louder. "I think I understand all that I need to understand."

I thought about slipping out the back door, then coming in noisily and interrupting them. But it was too late. My mom was in the kitchen doorway, flipping on the light switch.

"Joan, why are you sitting here in the dark?" my mom asked.

"I was working on my writing assignment," I said.

"Why didn't you turn on the light?"

"It was light enough." I stood up. With the kitchen light on, the window was like a mirror. I could no longer see the twilight sky, the backyard, the neighbor's cat. The window glass reflected our faces. My mom's face was pale and tense.

I gathered up my notebook and pen. "I'll go put this stuff away."

My mom had stepped into the kitchen, and my father was in the doorway. The room felt too small, too crowded.

I headed for my bedroom, moving quickly before I could be questioned further.

Not long after we had moved into the house, my mom had found a rocking chair at a yard sale. She had painted it white and sewed cushions for it. The cushions were covered in satin that was just the same color as the twilight sky. Royal blue, my mom called the color.

I sat in the rocking chair and looked into the backyard. I didn't turn on the bedroom light. Outside, the sky was fading to black. I opened the window a crack so that I could hear the crickets. Just a crack, so my father wouldn't accuse me of trying to air-condition the whole world.

Through the walls, I could hear my parents' voices. My father's voice rumbled like thunder—loud and angry, always angry. Sometimes he was yelling like the crash of thunder when the storm is right on top of you; sometimes he just talked low and mean, like the growling of a storm in the distance.

My mom's voice was softer. Sometimes her voice had a touch of pleading; sometimes, a touch of anger. Always softer than the rumbling thunder. More like leaves whispering in the storm winds. She was apologizing, always apologizing. I'm sorry you feel that way. I'm sorry . . . I'm sorry. What would happen if she stopped apologizing, I wondered.

I had a knot in my stomach.

For as long as I could remember, my father had complained about how much my mom spent, about how much things cost. It didn't seem fair. Lots of times, my mom bought stuff at garage sales and flea markets. When I was little, she made my clothes. She was smart enough to quit that when I started middle school, but she still bought store brands—nothing fancy.

I didn't ask for expensive gym shoes or stuff like that. I knew better. I wouldn't be part of the hip crowd even if I had designer clothes. I figured it was better to put up with occasional sneers from the kids with money than turn up the volume on my father's constant anger.

I tried to get back to my assignment from Verla. That was when I thought of something much scarier than spiders or ghosts or zombies: talking to my father about money.

*　　*　　*

"Did your parents ever argue?" I asked Fox the next morning. "Back when your mom was around."

Fox was lounging in the easy chair. I was sitting on the ground, leaning back against the tree. The day was hot and still.

"Oh, yeah," she said. "My mom used to throw things."

"She threw things? Like what?"

"Like plates and books and cups. Once she threw a pie across the room."

"Wow." Nobody threw anything at my house. "What did you do?"

"Tried to stay out of the way, mostly," she said. "Hid in another room and pretended I couldn't hear them." She shrugged. "It wasn't all that hard to do. They kind of forgot about me when they were fighting."

I nodded, remembering how easy it had been to sneak off to my room. "I think my parents went to see a marriage counselor last night," I said. "They came home arguing."

"Yeah? What were they arguing about?"

"Money. They always argue about money. My father says my mom spends too much."

Fox frowned. "I thought your father made a lot of money."

"I don't know how much money he makes. He never talks about money except to complain when my mom spends it."

"I'm sure he makes more money than my dad," Fox said.

"Yeah, I'm sure he does. But he was ragging on my mom about how she hadn't told him how much the writing class would cost." I hesitated. "Hey, do you know how much it costs?"

"I don't know, but my dad would know. We could ask."

Before I could stop her, she was up and heading for the house. I followed her reluctantly, not sure I wanted to bring Gus into this.

Gus was in the kitchen, working at his typewriter.

"Hey, Dad!" Fox said. "Can we ask you a question?"

He looked up from his work. For a moment, he didn't seem to see us—he was clearly thinking of something else. Then he focused on us. "Yeah. Right. In a couple of minutes, okay?"

"Okay," Fox said. "We'll be in the woods."

We walked back to the clearing. "He might forget," Fox said matter-of-factly. "Sometimes he does. Then I'll go remind him. And it'll probably be more than a couple of minutes. He can't keep track of time when he's writing."

I nodded. "Doesn't your dad get mad when you interrupt him like that? My dad would throw a fit."

"He used to. He'd stop what he was doing and help me right away, but he wouldn't be happy about it. Then we figured out that he could say he'd come see me when he could take a break. And that works okay most of the time."

"Does he ever yell at you? My dad yells all the time."

"Not much, anymore. He used to."

"How come he doesn't yell anymore?"

"I was kind of flunking out in school, after my mom went away. I had this teacher, Mrs. Miller. She made Dad come in and talk to her. And she yelled at him."

It was hard to imagine anyone yelling at Gus. "Really?"

"Yeah. She was this mean, little, old lady, and she sat us both down in the classroom and yelled at Dad about how he had to help me with my homework, and he had to create a stable home life, and all this stuff. I was sitting there listening, and then she yelled at me, too, telling me that this was a difficult time for Dad. She told me that I needed to stop acting like a brat." Fox shook her head, laughing. "Dad didn't say a word until later. Then he said, 'That's one scary teacher.'"

"What did you say?"

"I said, 'You got that right.' And then I said, 'It's not fun to get yelled at.'"

I nodded.

"So he got this funny look on his face and said, 'Yeah, I guess not.' And he told me that the next time he yelled at me, I should tell him that he sounded like Mrs. Miller."

"Wow. Did it work?"

Fox nodded. "It worked sometimes. And I think I sort of changed, too. It was weird—before Mrs. Miller yelled at him, I didn't really think of Dad as a person. I thought of him as more of a . . . sort of a dad-unit. This thing that orders you around and cooks dinner and tells you to go to bed."

I nodded. A dad-unit. That made sense. Not really a person. More like a force to be reckoned with, cajoled, avoided, fought against. That was how I'd been thinking of my mom—until Fox had interviewed her. She had been a mom-unit, an annoying entity that bugged me about things.

"After watching him get yelled at, he seemed like more of a person. And I tried to be better. I tried not to act like a brat. Then we got along better."

I heard the sound of a door slamming in the distance.

"Sounds like the dad-unit is on his way," Fox said, swinging her feet down to the ground.

Gus came down the path.

"Did you finish that story?" Fox asked.

"I finished the scene I was writing. So I'm good for a while." He sat on the ground by the tree. "So what's the question?"

"How much did the summer writing class at Berkeley cost?" Fox asked.

Gus frowned. "Why the sudden interest in high finance?"

"I hate it when you answer a question with a question," Fox said.

Gus waited for an answer.

"I wanted to know," I told Gus.

"Why?"

I hesitated, feeling uncomfortable.

"Can't you just tell us?" Fox asked Gus. "Do you have to know why?"

"I guess I don't have to know," Gus said. "The class cost two hundred and fifty dollars for the summer."

"Thanks," I said. Two hundred and fifty dollars was a lot of money, but I had that much. My uncle Ed, the one who had demanded my mother's dessert when they were kids, sent me twenty dollars every birthday and Christmas. I always saved that money. I'd earned some money back in Connecticut, watering our next-door neighbors' plants when they were on vacation. Last year, with my mom's help, I had opened a bank account. I had three hundred dollars in it.

Gus was watching me. "Is this something I could help with?" he asked.

I wondered how much to tell him, then decided he might have some good advice. I told him about my parents' fight. "They're always fighting about money," I said. "I thought I could pay for class myself so that they wouldn't be fighting about that."

"Were they fighting about that?" Gus asked.

"Yeah. My dad said the class cost too much, and my mom said it was important."

"Sounds like your mom was sticking up for you," Gus said.

"Yeah, I guess she was. Anyway, I really want to take the class. I thought I could pay for it myself. I have three hundred dollars in my bank account, so I could cover it."

Gus nodded. "It may not work," he said. "But it's worth a try."

"Why wouldn't it work?" Fox asked. "If he's mad about the money, this should fix it."

"It'll be great if it's that simple," Gus said. "But sometimes when people fight about money, it's not really the money that they're fighting about. You have to look for the subtext. That's something writers think about. Has Verla talked about that yet?"

Fox and I shook our heads.

"I bet she'll get to it soon. The text is what's happening on the surface. On the surface, your parents are fighting about money. The subtext is what's happening underneath."

"What do you mean?" Fox said.

"Money may not be the real issue," Gus said. "That's what they say they're fighting about, but the fight may really be about something else."

I thought about that. "My father starts talking about money whenever my mom does anything he doesn't like," I said slowly.

"Like what?"

"Like agreeing with the counselor that they'd been to see. Like saying that it was important that I go to the writing class. But I don't know what else they would be fighting about."

"Power," Gus said. "Lots of people use money as a symbol for power. Whoever controls the money controls the power."

I thought about my father and about how he always brought up money when my mom disagreed with him. As if money were a weapon that would make her agree.

I thought about money and power. Whoever controls the money, controls the power. If my father didn't want to pay for class, I could do it. I had enough money.

※ ※ ※

The bank had given me a checkbook when I got my bank account, but I'd never used it. After talking to Gus, Fox and I went to my house.

My mom was in the garden, and my father was at work. Fox and I got the checkbook out of the drawer in my desk where I kept it.

I had never written a check before, but I'd seen checks. Fox helped, and we figured out what should go where. Very carefully, I made a check out to my dad. Fox looked it over, making sure I hadn't missed anything. We were just finishing when my mom came in from the backyard, taking off her gardening gloves.

"Hey, girls, I was just going to have some lunch. Would you like some?"

"Sure," Fox said, standing up and following my mom into the kitchen.

I stuck the check into my back pocket and followed. My mom poured us each a glass of lemonade and made tuna-salad sandwiches. We all sat at the kitchen table.

"What are you up to today?" my mom asked. "Working on an assignment for writing class?"

Fox looked at me.

"Not exactly," I said slowly. I hesitated. I never talked to my mom about hearing her and my father fighting. She always pretended it hadn't happened, so I did the same. But I couldn't very well offer to pay for class without mentioning the fight. "I heard you and Dad talking about how much the writing class cost, and I thought I could pay for it. So I was writing a check for two hundred and fifty dollars. That's what the class cost, right?"

My mom got a strange expression on her face—kind of sad and angry at the same time. "Oh, that's silly. Your father doesn't need your two hundred and fifty dollars."

"He was saying that it cost too much," I said, my stomach tight.

"He was just kidding," she said.

That's what she did when my father gave her a hard time in front of us. She just pretended he was kidding. Usually, I went along with it. But this time I didn't.

"He didn't sound like he was kidding," I said. "I have the money. It's my money from my bank account. I'll give it to him, and then he can't complain about how much class costs."

My mom sighed. "Keep your money. Your father will just find something else to complain about."

It made me mad that she didn't think paying for class would do any good. "I just don't want him to keep talking about how I shouldn't go to class," I said.

"I'm sorry," my mom said.

I don't know what she was apologizing for. She hadn't done anything. And that made me mad, too.

My mom glanced at Fox, and I knew that she was

wondering what Fox thought of all this. Fox was finishing her sandwich, having eaten quietly while I talked with my mom.

"Would you like some more lemonade?" my mom asked Fox.

"Thank you," Fox said. I noticed that she was sitting up very straight and had her napkin politely in her lap. She was on her best behavior. "It's a very good sandwich."

While my mom was pouring Fox more lemonade, I wolfed the rest of my sandwich. As soon as we could, we escaped the house and went to the creek.

"Seems like your mom thought you might as well keep your money," Fox said as we walked along the railroad tracks on our way to the creek.

"Yeah," I said reluctantly. "Maybe."

"You don't really want to talk to your dad about this, do you?"

I scuffed my feet in the dirt. "You got that right. He's always mad about something."

"Your mom said he was joking about the money."

"She always says he's joking when he's being mean. He wasn't joking, and she knows it."

★ ★ ★

I had pretty much decided not to talk to my father about paying for the class. After all, my mom said it wouldn't do any good. Then my dad brought the class up while we were having dinner.

He started out ragging on Mark about mowing the

lawn. Mark had done the mowing but hadn't trimmed the grass around the flowerbeds. "You're trying for a new look? The untamed yard, right?"

Mark looked surly and kept eating his salad.

"This new look doesn't work for me," my father said.

"I'm sure Mark will have time to deal with that tomorrow," my mom said.

"He'll have time?" My father raised his eyebrows. "Well, I don't want to cut into his busy schedule. I'm sure he's very busy sleeping late and looking for trouble."

"I'm not sleeping late," Mark said. "I delivered newspapers this morning."

Mark had taken a summer job delivering newspapers in our neighborhood.

"Oh, that's right. I'd forgotten that you were working hard this summer. What is it—a grueling two or three hours a day? I'm surprised you have any time to mow the lawn at all!"

When Mark found the job delivering papers, I had thought my father would lighten up a little. But it hadn't worked. Now my father talked about how easy the job was. Dinner was almost over when he turned his attention to me.

"When do you go back to that summer class?" my father asked.

"Day after tomorrow," I said. "It's every Wednesday."

"So what do they have you doing there?" he said. "It must be pretty good considering what it costs."

"I'm learning to write." I kept my eyes on my plate.

"You already know how to write," my father said. "You won an award and everything. I don't see why you need to spend the summer hobnobbing with some university professor. It's a waste of time."

I noticed that my hand was in a fist in my lap. I was glad it was in my lap so my father couldn't see.

"It's a waste of money, too," my father said. "I don't know about paying good money so you can sit around and learn to be literary."

I looked up from my plate. I was mad. "You don't have to pay for it," I said.

My father looked surprised, just for a moment. He hesitated, frowning, and then said, "So you've decided not to take the class? I don't know if we can get that money back, just because you've changed your mind."

"I haven't changed my mind," I said. "But I can pay for the class myself." I still had the check I'd written in my back pocket. I took the check out and handed it to my father. "That will pay for my summer class," I said. Then I looked at my mom. "Could I be excused?"

Before my mom had a chance to say anything, while my father was still looking at the check, I escaped to my bedroom.

I was sitting in the rocking chair writing in my notebook when someone knocked on my door. Thinking it was my mom, I yelled, "Come in."

It was my father. "I want to talk to you," he said.

I didn't know what to say, so I didn't say anything. I stared at him, waiting for him to say something sarcastic and mean.

He sat on the edge of the bed. He was holding the check I had given him. "Why did you give me this?" he asked.

For a moment, I didn't say anything. I could have said, "To pay for summer class," but that would have sounded like I was being a smart-ass. I had already called enough attention to myself. Finally I said, "Writing class isn't a waste of money. I need to learn about writing."

"Why is that?"

For once, he was asking questions and waiting for the answers. He didn't seem to be joking or being mean. "I'm writing a book," I said. I didn't know where those words came from. I had to say something and that was what I said.

"A book," my father repeated. "I see." He looked thoughtful, maybe a little impressed. Then he looked at the check in his hand. "Did your mother put you up to this?"

I shook my head, amazed that he hadn't made a mean joke about the idea of me writing a book. "It was my idea. I told her, and she tried to talk me out of it."

"Where did you get the idea?" he asked.

"I heard you and Mom arguing about how much class cost," I said.

My father nodded. He had an odd expression. I guess he never thought much about me listening to him and Mom argue. "What are you learning in this class?" he asked.

"I'm learning to ask questions," I said.

He stared at me. "Like what?"

I looked at the check in his hand. "If you had ten thousand dollars and you had to spend it in the next hour, what would you buy?"

"I'd put it in my savings account," my father said.

"You can't do that," I said. "You have to spend it. What would you buy?"

I waited while my father frowned at me. "That's a strange question," he said.

"Why?" I had learned Gus's trick of answering a question with a question.

"Because that's not the way things work," he said. "I don't have to spend ten thousand dollars right now." He looked at the check in his hand. "But I suppose if I did, I'd spend part of it on this class so you can write this book." He looked at me. "I didn't know this class thing was so important to you. I thought it was just another one of your mother's harebrained schemes." He put the check down on my bed. "You keep this, okay? You go to class."

11

CIRCUS OF CHAOS

"What did you write about?" I asked Fox the next day. I hadn't written my second assignment yet, and I only had one day left.

She looked uncomfortable. "Talking in front of a bunch of people," she said, a little sheepishly.

I nodded slowly. I knew she didn't like that. When it came to doing some things, she was fearless: she'd catch a snake or walk through a dark culvert. But she wasn't so good with people.

"You did fine when we read our story," I said.

"That's because we were wearing war paint," she said. "It wasn't really me. I was hiding behind the war paint."

That made sense. I had felt the same way. The lipstick war paint had changed us into the wild girls, and the wild girls weren't afraid of anything.

"What are you writing about?" she asked me.

"I don't know. I can't come up with anything. I tried writing about talking with my dad—that was scary. But it didn't seem like the right kind of scary."

"I felt kind of stupid writing about being scared of talking in front of a crowd," Fox said. "But it was something that really scared me. What really scares you?"

I recognized that question. It was one of the questions Verla had written on the board. "If I could figure that out, I could write something," I said, a little annoyed.

"If you don't know the answer, make something up," she said. That was something else Verla said.

"Okay, then—spiders." I did think spiders were creepy.

"Why?"

"Because they have too many legs."

"What else scares you?"

"Monsters."

"What kind of monsters?"

"The kind with lots of sharp teeth. They used to hide in my closet when I was a little kid."

She nodded as if she knew those monsters. "What else scares you?" She acted like she was going to keep on asking the same question forever.

"Listening to my mom and dad fight," I said.

"Yeah? Why does that scare you?"

I bit my lip, feeling like I had said more than I should. Listening to my parents argue made my stomach hurt, made me hide in my room. It really did scare me. I didn't know why, exactly. But I could make something up. "Because my father turns into one of those monsters that hide in the closet," I said. "The kind with big teeth."

Fox sat up straight in the easy chair, suddenly grinning. "Now *that's* scary," she said.

I nodded slowly. "I remember hearing my mom tell him, 'You don't have to bite my head off.'"

"A monster with sharp teeth and a really big mouth," Fox said.

✳ ✳ ✳

At the beginning of the next class, Verla collected our papers. Then a guy from the university library came in and told us about how we could get a library card there if we wanted. He talked about how important it was to do research. While he was talking, people kept fidgeting in their seats and glancing at the back of the class, where Verla was reading our papers.

Finally, he was done, and Verla got up in front of the class again.

"Today, I'm going to read some of your work aloud," Verla said. "Then we'll talk about what works in it and what doesn't."

By people's expressions, I guessed I wasn't the only one who was terrified by that idea. But Verla wasn't looking at people's expressions. She was leafing through the papers, choosing one to read.

She picked one from the stack and began to read: "'What do you like for breakfast?' I asked my dad. 'Corned beef hash on toast,' he said."

It could have been anyone's paper, anyone's dad. But I was sitting just behind Zoom. I couldn't see her face, but I could see her left ear poking out a bit because she'd tucked her hair behind it. By the second sentence, her ear had turned bright red. She was blushing. It had to be her paper.

I remember she had said her father was a minister, so I expected him to talk about the Bible and stuff like that. But she didn't ask him about the Bible. If he had to spend ten thousand dollars, he would buy more milk goats and cheese-making equipment for the orphanage that their church sponsored in Atlixco, Mexico.

She asked him what alias he would choose, if he had to choose an alias. She said she'd decided to be Zoom. He said that maybe he'd be Zoomdaddy. After all, when she became the famous writer Zoom, he'd want everyone to know that she was his daughter.

I had always thought that being a minister would be really dull—sitting around reading the Bible all the time. But Zoom's father sounded really nice. It made me feel a little funny listening to her interview, though. I didn't think Zoom would ever be scared of her father.

Verla talked awhile about how you could learn a lot about someone by asking simple questions. She asked other people what they thought, but nobody really had much to say. I think we were all wondering whose paper she'd read next. Zoom's ear was still very red.

"What did you think of the guy in this interview?" Verla asked. Nobody raised a hand. "Come on," Verla said. "Wake up. Somebody must have an opinion."

We were plenty awake, I thought. I could feel my heart pounding. I wanted to be invisible so that Verla wouldn't call on me. I wanted to take my papers back so Verla couldn't read them aloud.

"Al," Verla said. "What do you think of this guy?"

Al looked up, startled. He had been doodling in his notebook. "He seemed like a nice guy," Al said.

"Why is that?"

Al glanced at Zoom. "He's buying goats to help other people."

"Bodie," Verla said. "Do you agree?"

I kept an eye on Zoom. Gradually, as people talked about how nice her dad was, her ear faded from bright red to dull red, and then to a more normal ear color.

Just when I was starting to relax, Verla pulled another paper from the stack and started to read. It took me a minute to realize that Verla was reading from Fox's interview with my mother. In the version Fox had written, my mom was a lonely queen, locked in a castle tower. I recognized her as the mother of the princess who had become one of the wild girls. Fox and I had talked about the queen, but we'd never written much about her. The queen, it turned out, had grown up on a farm and raised pumpkins.

"Joan, what do you think?" Verla asked.

"Well, I know Fox didn't really interview a queen in a castle."

Verla nodded. "I suspect that's the case. She did an

interview, and then used her imagination. What else do you think?"

"I liked it."

"Why?"

I looked at Fox, looked at my hands. "When the queen talked about growing pumpkins, you knew she didn't belong in the castle."

Verla frowned a little. "Is that what you know?"

I stared at her, not knowing what to say.

"You know she didn't grow up in the castle," Zoom piped up. "You know she doesn't feel like she belongs there."

I smiled at Zoom, grateful that she had bailed me out.

Verla nodded. "When you're talking to a character, you find out what they think and feel. But what a character feels isn't always true."

Verla talked for a while about characters and how they could say things that weren't quite true or could lie outright. I wasn't really listening. I was watching the clock, thinking that we would get out for lunch before she had a chance to read anything else.

I was wrong. "Your other assignment was to write about something scary," she said. Then she pulled another paper from the stack and started to read:

"At night, I hear my father growling as he prowls the house, sniffing at the bedroom doors. I keep my door locked."

I slumped down in my chair, wishing I were behind that locked bedroom door right then. She read it all: the fight where my parents argued about money and where my mom said, "You don't have to bite my head off." I could feel my face getting hot, and I could only hope that my ears hadn't turned as red as Zoom's had.

I couldn't listen to the discussion that followed. Verla called on people and they said stuff, but I was looking down at my hands, wanting to be somewhere else, anywhere else. When Verla finally said it was lunchtime, I was the first one out of the room.

Fox caught up with me just outside the door. "That was great," she said.

"I didn't know she was going to read stuff out loud," I said. My face was still hot and my heart was pounding so hard I figured everyone could hear it. "I feel like an idiot."

"What a character feels isn't always true," Bodie said. He had come up behind Fox. Zoom and Al were just behind him.

I glared at Bodie, who was grinning. "Who asked you?"

"You don't have to bite my head off," he said, and his grin widened. "Just relax."

"Easy for you to say." I knew my face was still red. "Wait till she reads *your* stuff out loud."

Al, who was standing just behind Bodie, shook his head. "That won't bother him a bit," Al said.

Bodie shrugged. "Everyone already thinks I'm an idiot.

One story isn't going to change public opinion, one way or the other."

Al nodded. "He's right about that."

Bodie just kept grinning. "Want to go to Sproul Plaza for lunch? It's a lot better and cheaper than the deli," he said. "And the Circus of Chaos is going to be there."

"What's the Circus of Chaos?" Zoom asked.

"Come on. You'll see."

"Okay," Fox said. When she and Zoom followed Bodie and Al, I went along.

I walked beside Zoom. Fox was a little bit ahead, walking with Bodie and Al. As we walked, my heart gradually stopped beating so hard.

"Your story was really scary," Zoom said as we walked.

"Yeah?"

"Yeah. Even before the father turns into a monster, it was scary," she said. "Like one of those movies where you know something really bad is going to happen, and you don't know what."

I nodded, happy to hear that she didn't think it was stupid. "I liked your interview with your dad," I told her.

She nodded, smiling shyly. "My mom and dad have started calling me Zoom," she said. "I really like it."

I smiled for the first time since Verla had read my story. "That's good."

Bodie led us over a broad bridge that spanned a small creek. I could hear rhythmic music in the distance—bells, rattles, drums of different sizes. We stepped through an arched iron gateway wide enough for a dozen people to walk through side by side. Bodie headed toward the sound of the drums.

"This is one of the best places on campus," Bodie said. "There's always something going on here. All the student groups have tables where they hand out fliers and stuff. Circus of Chaos has a table."

The drummers sat in a circle, some on a bench, some on the brick-paved plaza. Halfway across the plaza, a stilt walker danced to the music. She must have been eight feet tall. She wore a bright fuchsia T-shirt that stood out against the sky, and she trailed gauzy pink scarves from both hands. She wore dark blue pants that reached all the way to the ground, so it didn't look like she was on stilts. It looked like she had really, really long legs. Her face was painted—half bright pink, half deep blue. On the deep-blue half were golden stars. Her long hair was in dozens of tight braids, each one tipped with a bead that glittered in the sun. Her braids swung wildly as she danced to the beat of the drums.

Not far from her, a woman wearing a T-shirt that said CIRCUS OF CHAOS sat at a card table in the shade of a tree. Her face was painted with a pattern of silver and iridescent-blue shapes, arranged like overlapping scales. Her blue eyes were startling in the center of a swath of silver scales edged with black.

The sign that hung from the table said in large red letters: JOIN THE CIRCUS OF CHAOS. Below that, in smaller black type, it said: JUGGLING, STILT WALKING, BALLOON SCULPTURE, AND OTHER SKILLS FOR SOCIALLY ACCEPTABLE PROCRASTINATION.

The woman smiled when she saw Bodie approaching. "Hey, Bodie! What are you up to?"

"We're on lunch break. These are my friends. I thought they might want to try walking on stilts."

Walking on stilts? He hadn't mentioned that before.

The woman smiled at us. "I'm Azalea." When we introduced ourselves, she didn't seem startled by Fox's name or Zoom's name. "I could show one person how to use the handheld stilts. It would take longer to introduce you to the peg stilts that a professional stilt walker uses." She gestured to a pair of stilts lying on the pavement by the table. "Bodie, you can help yourself to those if you like. I know you can handle them."

Bodie picked up the stilts. He sat down on the low cement wall that ringed the shade tree and strapped the stilts onto his feet.

"Need a hand up?" the woman said.

"Sure."

She placed her foot on the rubber-tipped feet of the stilts, grabbed Bodie's hand, and leaned back, pulling him up. Before we could say a word he was four feet taller. "It gives you a whole new perspective on the world," he said, looking down at us. He swayed a bit, and then took a step toward the dancing stilt walker. Al followed, looking up at Bodie.

I watched him, startled. The rhythm of the drums filled the air, a syncopated beat that made me feel like dancing, too.

Fox's eyes were shining. "That's cool!" she said, staring at Bodie and the stilt walker. In her excitement, she had forgotten to be shy.

"Those are peg stilts. Takes a lot of practice to use those. Bodie's been here before. But you can try the handhelds if you want," Azalea said.

A few minutes later, Fox was up on a pair of stilts. Hers were shorter and simpler than the ones that Bodie was using. His seemed like extensions of his legs. Fox's stilts were a pair of poles with footrests. She stood on the footrests and held the poles. Soon, she was striding across the plaza toward Bodie and the dancer, leaving Zoom and me with Azalea.

"I'm out of stilts," she said.

"That's okay," I said, and it really was okay. I wasn't so sure I wanted to try the stilts. "Some other time."

"I could paint your faces, if you like," she said. "A few strokes of the brush and you'll be transformed."

I hesitated, remembering the lipstick war paint at the reading. I remembered the feeling of power and anonymity I had felt onstage.

Azalea was studying me. "What's your totem animal?"

She asked the question so naturally, as if everyone had a totem animal and everyone knew what that totem animal was.

If you don't know the answer, make something up, Verla had said. The first thing I'd heard when I woke up that morning was the mockingbird singing—and ringing like a telephone and hooting like an owl. "The mockingbird," I said.

"Ah," she said, "I like that." She took a box from beneath the table. "If I remember right, the mockingbird is gray with a startling flash of white on its wings."

"That's right," I said.

"It looks like an unassuming bird," she said, opening the box and taking out tubes of paint and a paint-smeared piece of white tile, about one-foot square. "But then it sings. Or it takes flight and you see these wonderful flashes of white on its wings." She dabbed some black paint and some white paint on the tile, then used a fat brush to mix them, creating a smear of gray that ranged from nearly white to nearly black. "Close your eyes."

I hadn't said that she could paint my face. I simply closed my eyes.

"The Hopi say that the singing of a mockingbird guided the first people from the darkness to the light," Azalea said. The brush was cool against my face, gently stroking my skin. "A mockingbird in the tree near my dorm teases one of the dorm cats. The bird meows like a cat, and the cat looks around for the other cat. I think it's the bird's idea of a joke. Pretty brave, for a bird—don't you think? Teasing a cat like that."

I didn't say anything, but Azalea kept talking; she didn't seem to need my help.

"That bird can imitate anything. It likes to make the sound of a telephone ringing. People walking by look around, wondering where the phone is. Mockingbirds like to play."

I wondered if the mockingbird that sang on the chimney every morning was teasing my father. The brush tickled my chin, my cheek, my forehead.

"The tough thing about being a mockingbird is figuring out your own song," Azalea said. "That's what I think. Too many songs to sing. How do you know which one is your own?"

Another brush, a smaller one, traced patterns around my eyes.

"I like painting feathers," Azalea said. "All lightness and air. Just the thing for summer."

I didn't have to answer. Of course she was right. I felt lighter with each stroke of the brush, as if my solid bones were becoming hollow bird bones, as if my clothes were becoming feathers.

"Very nice," she said at last. "All done."

I opened my eyes. Azalea took a pocket mirror from the box and held it up for me. I looked into the face of a stranger—a very strange stranger. A girl with a face of feathers—many shades of gray, touches of yellow near the eyes, a patch of white at each temple.

"Dignified, I think," Azalea said. "Elegant and dignified."

I stared at the girl in the mirror who blinked when I blinked, bit her lip when I bit my lip.

"Do you know your own song?" Azalea asked.

"I'm learning," I said.

*　*　*

We rushed back to class, carrying pita-bread sandwiches that we had bought at one of the food wagons. Fox's face was painted in red and brown streaks—not a fox, but borrowing the colors of a fox. She had seen my face and had insisted on having her own painted as well. Zoom asked Azalea to paint her face to match her new name. Zoom's face was silver with lightning bolts in black and gold. Al's face was patterned like a snakeskin, in honor of Mr. Squeeze.

Bodie said his totem animal was the clown. Azalea said that circus clowns were boring, but she could paint him like a Hopi clown. As she painted his face white, with black around the eyes and mouth, she told us that she had spent last summer in Arizona, working with the Hopi tribe on the reservation.

As we hurried back to class, people were smiling at us, laughing, pointing us out to their friends. I felt like I had when I was wearing lipstick war paint—I was in disguise and I could do anything.

We made it back just as Verla was calling the class to order. She smiled at us. I smiled back. When I left class, I had been really mad at her for reading my story. But that seemed like a long time ago.

"I see you made excellent use of your lunch hour," Verla said. "Circus of Chaos, right? I recognize Azalea's work."

I nodded. Of course she knew about Circus of Chaos. I glanced at Fox. I felt like I had entered a secret world. Walk through the right gate, and you'd find amazing people and wondrous creatures. And of course Verla would know all about them.

"Time for some more reading," Verla said.

She read a story that Al had written. I knew it was Al's because it was about a snake named Mr. Squeeze. "Mr. Squeeze loves my sister's little kitten," Verla read. "He wants to hug her very hard. He wants to love that kitten to death."

Verla read a story by Matthew about zombies that lived in the school cafeteria, dishing up the food, and a story by Ketura about getting stuck at the top of a Ferris wheel. We talked about them all. Fox raised her hand and commented on the stories. With her fox face painted on, it was easier for her to talk about other people's stories. We were the wild girls, and we had a lot to say.

Finally, Verla gave us our next assignment.

"This one's hard," she said. "I want you to write something that's true."

"About what?" Al asked.

"Whatever you want," Verla said. "You can write a description of something. You can write a conversation with someone. You can write a letter that you don't plan to send. I'll give you a list of ideas to use in case you get stumped. But you can write about anything you want. As long as there's truth in it."

Tyler frowned. "I thought we were writing fiction," he said. "I thought we were making things up."

Verla smiled. "You are. And that's where it gets really interesting," she said. "Any liar can make things up. But a good writer is more than just a clever liar. A good writer tells the truth by telling lies."

PART THREE
LEARNING TO FLY

12

AN UNEXPECTED LETTER

When I went to Fox's the next day, she wasn't in the clearing. So I went down the path to her house.

Their front door was open. The house had a crappy old air conditioner, the kind that took up half a window. They usually didn't bother using it. Walnut trees shaded the house. Gus left all the windows and doors open and sometimes turned on an electric fan "to move the hot air around," he said.

Their house was hot and messy and kind of crowded, but I liked it anyway. At my house, I couldn't leave things lying around without my mom asking me to clean up. Fox and I could leave our stuff in the clearing or on the porch for days, and Gus wouldn't even notice. Because the house was small, Fox and I spent most of our time out in the clearing. I liked that.

Fox was sitting at the kitchen table, opening letters. "Come on in!" she called when she saw me. "I'm checking my dad's fan mail for him. Every month or so, his publisher sends him an envelope full. He ignores it mostly, but every once in a while, I sort through it for him, looking for the good stuff."

I looked over Fox's shoulder. "What's the good stuff?"

She shrugged. "I can't tell you exactly, but I know it when I see it. Here's a guy who's complaining that Dad got the physics wrong in a story. That's not the good stuff. I'll put that in a folder for Dad to look at when he has time. Like never, most likely. I tell Dad that he should write back to everyone, but he never does."

Fox put the offending letter on the table, picked up another envelope from the stack in front of her, and tore it open. "Here's someone who loved Dad's last novel. That's good stuff. I'll show that one to him right away."

She set that one on the table beside the first letter.

"Once I found a letter from some guy who wanted to pay Dad a thousand dollars to teach at a writers' workshop."

"That's great."

"Yeah," Fox said as she opened another envelope. "It's like a treasure hunt. You never know . . ." Then she stopped talking and just stared at the letter in her hand. Her eyes had widened.

"What is it?" I asked. "What have you found?"

I looked over her shoulder and read the letter.

Dear Gus, it began. *I've written this letter in my head a thousand times and it never comes out right. I guess it will never come out right, and that's just the way it is.*

"It's a letter from Mom," Fox said, her voice tiny.

Have you ever had one of those moments where everything changes? You're going along and everything's normal—then something happens, and it's like the air crys-
tallizes or something. Everything comes into sharp focus.
You pay attention to everything—every little detail.

I remember Fox's face. She looked like someone who
had just been handed an impossible puzzle, and she was
trying to work it out.

Fox and I read the letter, not saying anything at all.
Here's what it said:

Dear Gus,

*I've written this letter in my head a thousand times and it never
comes out right. I guess it will never come out right, and that's just
the way it is.*

*Five years ago, I walked out the door and caught a Greyhound
bus. I bought a ticket to Portland, Oregon—not because I wanted
to go to Portland, but because I wanted to run away from San Francisco. I bought a bottle of vodka to drink on the bus, and I sat in the
back and drank and cried as that bus headed north.*

Why did I leave?

*I left because I couldn't stop drinking. I left because I thought
you and Sarah would be better off without me. I left because I was
selfish. I left because of a calico cat I had when I was nine years old.*

*That calico cat was an alley cat, out every night prowling
around and looking for trouble. Then she had kittens, cute little
balls of fur with big innocent eyes. Sometimes she would nurse those
kittens. But sometimes when they tried to snuggle up and nurse,*

she would hiss and swat at them, no matter how they cried.

I tried to keep the cat inside when she was nursing the kittens. But anytime the door was open for a second, she would go streaking out. She'd be out all night, while her kittens wandered around the house looking for her and crying. She'd come home, and sometimes she'd lie down and let her kittens nurse and be with her. Then she'd change her mind and go out again. Those poor kittens cried all the time. One day, she left and never came back.

Just before I left, I remember thinking that I was like that cat. Sometimes, I would read Sarah a bedtime story and sing her a song—and sometimes I would yowl and spit and get drunk. And she would look at me with those big, sad eyes, and that just made me pour another drink.

The day that I left, I washed the dishes and put them away. I cleaned the house. And all the time I was doing it, I was thinking about that cat. Then I went to the Greyhound station. I didn't really have a plan. I was like that cat. I was a bad mom and I just left.

I won't tell you all the things that I've been doing for the past five years. It would take a long time, and many of those things are worth remembering only to remind myself not to do them again. But here's where I am now:

It has been two years since I've had a drink. I attend Alcoholics Anonymous meetings regularly. It isn't easy staying sober, but it's better than getting drunk.

In Alcoholics Anonymous, I have a sponsor, a woman named Karen. Karen told me to make a list of all the people I'd hurt. You and Sarah are at the top of that list.

Then Karen said I should make amends to those people wherever

I could. The only reason not to make amends is if doing so would injure those people even more.

Making amends means more than just apologizing. It means taking action to clear up problems from the past. It means explaining what happened and asking forgiveness. It means paying back what I owe.

I want to make amends. I think about you and Sarah every day. I want to talk to you. I don't know if talking to Sarah would injure her even more, but if you think it would be okay, I'd like to talk to Sarah.

Please write back so that I know you have received this letter, even if all you can say is: "I got your message."

Love,

Nita

There was a P.S. that said *Here's my phone number if you want to call,* and gave a phone number.

✳   ✳   ✳

"She disappeared when I was seven," Fox said. This was a little later, after we had read the letter over again, three or four times. We were still sitting at the table. Fox looked stunned and confused.

"That was when we still lived in San Francisco, in this little apartment. My friend Suzy lived down the block, and Suzy's mom usually came and got us at school and walked us home. That day, no one was at my house when we got there. That happened sometimes." Fox was staring at nothing. "So I went home with Suzy, and later on,

Foxes mom
is not
a Fox

Dad came over and got me. He was working for a moving company, loading trucks and stuff. He picked me up
at Suzy's, and he was pissed off." Fox looked down at her
hands. "He was pissed off a lot, back then. Mom drank a
lot and Dad drank sometimes, too. He quit that a while
after Mom disappeared."

She frowned, remembering. "When we got home, it
was weird. The place wasn't a mess, the way it usually was.
Usually, Mom's clothes were all over the place. But her
clothes were gone. There weren't any dishes in the sink.
They were all washed and put away. The kitchen was clean.
But my mom wasn't home."

"Was there a note or anything?" I asked.

Fox shook her head.

"So what did your dad do?"

"Called a bunch of friends to see if they knew where
she was. He thought she might be out somewhere getting
drunk," Fox said. She was watching me, as if waiting for
my reaction. "When he couldn't find her, he told me that
she'd be home later that night. I figured she would come
home and they'd have a big fight like they always did and
then stuff would go on the way it always had."

I had seen Gus angry the time my brother and his pals
had pulled down the shelves in the walnut tree. That had
been scary. I imagined him and Fox's mom, a shadowy figure with fox-colored hair who liked to throw things, fighting in a tiny apartment while Fox tried to stay out of the
way. My stomach hurt. I felt like I couldn't move or talk.

"But Mom didn't show up the next day. None of her friends knew where she was. Dad called the cops and told them that she was missing. He went down to the police station and filed a missing-persons report. We put up posters all around the neighborhood, asking if anyone had seen her. And we checked with the cops all the time for a while. But we never found out anything about where she went."

"So what did you do?"

"I just kept going to school. And I did really lousy. After Mom disappeared, I didn't care about anything. That was when my teacher—Mrs. Miller—yelled at Dad.

"So he started going to Alcoholics Anonymous meetings. I stayed late at school those days, helping Mrs. Miller with stuff."

"I thought she was really scary," I said.

"Only when she was mad. The rest of the time, she was okay. Anyway, Dad kept working for the moving company, but he kept on writing stories, too. He had always been writing stories. Finally, he sold one. I remember that. When he got home from work, there was a letter in the mail with a contract in it. This magazine wanted to buy the story. Dad and I went out on his motorcycle and got burgers and milk shakes to celebrate. It was winter and it was raining, but it was warm in the burger joint, and Dad was talking about how this was the first step, the beginning of good stuff. He was right about that. His story won a prize for being the best science-fiction story that year, and he sold a bunch more stories.

"We moved out of the city a year or so later. Dad's uncle owned this place, and we'd come and visit Uncle George every week or so. Then Uncle George died, and he left this place to Dad. So we moved out here. I worried that Mom wouldn't be able to find us if she came back, but Dad said she could find us if she wanted to. Dad sold a novel that he'd written, and he didn't work for the moving company anymore." She shrugged. "Stuff was better, and we never heard from Mom. I figured we never would."

"But now you have."

Fox stared at the letter. "Yeah. She gave Dad her phone number." Fox was starting to sound more like herself. "I could call her."

"I don't know," I said. "Shouldn't you wait and talk to your dad first?"

"She's my mom. I can talk to her if I want." Now she definitely sounded like herself. She was mad, and she wanted to do something.

"What are you going to say?"

"I'm going to ask her questions. I want to know where she's been, what she's been doing."

I tended to think about things for a long time before I did them. Fox was the opposite. While I was still thinking of objections, she picked up the phone. Her face was pale. Her mouth was stretched into a thin, tight line. She punched the numbers into the phone.

"Hello," she said into the phone. Her voice was unsteady. "Hello, Mom? I wanted to talk to you." Then, all of a sudden, she was crying. "I wanted to . . . I wanted to . . ."

But she couldn't finish the sentence. Her words were caught in her throat.

I reached out to touch her shoulder, to reassure her. She handed me the phone and buried her face in her hands.

I held the phone to my ear.

"Sarah!" The woman's voice was frantic. "Are you all right? What's going on?"

"This is Joan," I said. "I'm Fox's . . . I mean, I'm Sarah's friend."

"Is Sarah all right?"

"Sarah's upset," I said. I was furious with this woman. How could she leave Fox and then just show up again? "She has some questions for you."

"Okay," said Fox's mother. "Okay. Can I talk to Sarah?"

"No," I said. I was angry, and she was a voice on the phone, nothing more. It's easier to be rude to someone on the phone than it is to be rude to someone in person. "You can't talk to her. She's upset. I'll ask questions for her."

Fox had taken her hands away from her face. Her hands were in fists, but she didn't look like she could talk. She had wanted to ask questions. I tried to think of what questions to ask for her. This didn't seem like the right time to ask her favorite color or what she had for breakfast. "She wants to know why you left," I said.

"Where's Gus?" Fox's mother asked. "Is he there?"

"Gus isn't here now," I told her. "Sarah was going through his mail for him, and we found your letter."

"When's Gus coming back?"

I was getting mad. Rather than answering me, she kept asking her own questions. I decided not to answer her question. "They thought you might be dead, you know," I said.

"What I did was terrible. I'm sorry for that. Can I please talk to Sarah?"

I heard the roar of Gus's motorcycle, coming down the drive to the house.

"I can hear your dad coming," I said to Fox. I knew we shouldn't have called Fox's mother, and now we were caught. "What should we do?"

Fox reached out and without hesitation hung up the phone, cutting her mother off. Then Gus walked in, carrying a bag of groceries. "They had a great deal on strawberries," he was saying as he walked in the door.

Then he saw Fox's face, and he stopped. "What's going on?" he asked.

"We got a letter from Mom," Fox said.

He stared at her. "From Nita?" he asked. His voice was low, barely above a whisper, and he sounded like he didn't believe it. He came to the table and read the letter over Fox's shoulder. I pushed my chair back, giving him room. He was a big guy, and right then he seemed even bigger.

He read the letter once. Then he pulled up a chair, sat

down, picked up the letter, and read it again. His expression was blank, unreadable, and a little bit scary.

He looked at Fox. "So should I call her?"

Fox looked at me, then looked back at Gus. "I already did."

Gus scowled. "You did."

Fox nodded, looking very small.

Gus looked back at the letter. Then he spoke slowly. "Why did you call her?"

Fox didn't say anything, so I spoke up. "Fox was going to ask her some questions. Interview her, like we did for class."

Gus looked incredulous. "That would be an interesting interview. What did you ask?"

Fox didn't say anything, so I answered again. "We didn't get very far. I asked why she left. She said that what she did was terrible. She said that she should never have left."

"What else?" Gus asked.

I looked at Fox. "I don't know. We hung up when we heard you coming."

"You hung up on her? That serves her right, I guess."

I noticed that his hands were in fists. His shoulders were tense. I could see all the muscles in his arms. He looked like he wanted to hit someone.

"What are you going to do?" Fox asked.

"First I'm going to sit here and stew for a while. Then I'll decide what to do."

Fox nodded. "How long do you think you need to stew?"

Gus shrugged. "A couple of hours, at least. I spent a couple of years forgiving her. I read all this stuff about how forgiveness is really important, that the only one you hurt by holding on to resentment is yourself. I thought I had forgiven her. But I was wrong about that."

"Maybe we should get out of here while you stew," Fox said, standing up.

★ ★ ★

We went to the creek. Actually, we fled. Just then, Gus seemed to fill the entire house. He wasn't doing anything, but it was difficult to be in the same room with him. So we left him at the kitchen table, reading the letter over again. I don't think he really noticed when we left.

When we got to the creek, Fox sat on the bank and I sat beside her.

"How are you doing?" I asked.

"I don't know," she said slowly. "I'd gotten used to having a mother who was a fox."

"Yeah. Must be weird to talk to her after all these years."

Fox's face was frozen, unreadable. "Right after she left, sometimes I'd get really mad at her. And then afterward, I'd be sorry, because I thought maybe she'd been kidnapped or murdered or something. So I'd feel bad that I'd been mad. But then I'd think that maybe she hadn't been kidnapped. I wondered if maybe she'd left because I wasn't a good kid."

I put my hand on her shoulder. I didn't know what to say.

"I was really mean to my mom sometimes," she said slowly. "She'd get drunk and I'd get mad at her." She looked at me and tried to smile. It was a weak, watery kind of smile. "A couple of days before she left, I was watching a Road Runner cartoon on TV. She had a headache and she made me turn it off. She said, 'If I hear that stupid bird say *beep beep* one more time, my head's going to explode.' Then she turned off the TV. I was so mad I screamed, 'I hate you. I hate you.' Maybe that's why she left."

"I don't think she'd leave because of that," I said.

"How do you know?"

"She didn't say anything about that in her letter," I said. "She didn't say that when we asked her."

"Maybe," Fox said. "But right after she left, sometimes I'd think it was my fault. Then I'd decide it wasn't, and I'd get mad at her all over again." She shook her head. "Finally I decided that she'd turned into a fox. That seemed like the best thing." She sighed. "But it turns out she wasn't a fox at all. So I can feel myself getting mad and getting sad and getting scared."

"I thought you were really brave to call her."

Fox frowned. "I figured I had to. Thanks for talking to her when I couldn't."

"You didn't have to call her. You could just have left the letter for your dad and let him figure out what to do."

Fox didn't say anything for a minute. She just stared at the water in the creek. Then she said, "Remember the time we walked all the way through the culvert?"

"Of course. I'll never forget that." It had been terrifying and really cool at the same time.

"It was like that," she said. "I felt like I had to. Once I knew I could call her, I just had to keep going." She looked at me. "You know, I never could have walked all the way through the culvert if you hadn't come along."

I stared at her. "I didn't do anything." I had followed her that day, doing my best not to freak out. That was all I did.

"I knew that if anything happened, you would be there to help," she said.

I stared at her, surprised. Fox usually acted like she didn't need any help at all. But now she sounded uncertain, like she wanted to know that I wasn't going to run out on her.

"Sure," I said. "If I can help, I'll do it." I hesitated, and then added, "As long as I can figure out what to do."

✦ ✦ ✦

It was late afternoon when we went back to Fox's house. Gus was sitting on the porch steps, drinking a soda and looking out at the woods. "I was starting to wonder what happened to you two," Gus said. "It's past five. You usually head home before five, don't you, Newt?"

After five? "I'll see you later," I told Fox, and headed home.

I got home at five thirty, knowing I was in trouble. At five thirty, Mom was usually bustling around the kitchen, getting dinner ready. I was supposed to get home by five, so I could set the table. Unless my father was on a business trip, he got home at quarter to six or so, and we ate at six. That was the way it always was.

But the house was quiet. I looked in the kitchen: clean white counter, sink empty of dishes. Mom wasn't there.

There was a piece of notebook paper on the dining-room table. It was folded over, and my name was written on the outside in Mom's handwriting. I looked at it for a minute, feeling really strange.

I didn't know if I wanted to open it. But I unfolded the note. It said:

I'm at the community college. There's lasagna for dinner. It's in the fridge. Put it in the oven at 350° for half an hour. Serve it with the tossed salad. I'll be back at 10. Mom.

I remembered then. Mom was taking a class on landscape design at the local junior college. She had told me about it. I'd forgotten that she was starting this week.

I looked in the refrigerator and saw the lasagna and salad. I put the lasagna in the oven and turned it on to 350°.

My brother was in his room, reading a science-fiction novel with an exploding spaceship on the cover.

"Hey," I said, "Mom's taking a class tonight."

"Yeah. I know. I heard her and Dad fighting about it yesterday."

"Yeah?"

"Dad was going on about how it was a big waste of time. Mom said it wasn't and she was going to take it anyway. I bet they'll talk about it in marriage counseling."

So he knew about the marriage counseling, too. "Do you think that will do any good?" I asked.

My brother made a face. "Not a chance. Dad isn't going to listen to some stupid quack." Mark did a good job of imitating my father's voice on the last couple of words. My father always called doctors "quacks." "He's going to say it's too expensive and stop going."

I nodded. That sounded pretty likely. I glanced at the clock. It was around six. "Shouldn't Dad be home by now?"

"He called and said he was going out with some people from work. Said we should eat dinner without him."

My brother got some lasagna and took it back to his room so he could keep reading while he ate. I served myself some lasagna and salad and ate at the kitchen table. I was hungry—Fox and I had forgotten about lunch.

I went to my bedroom. Mark had turned the air-conditioning way up, and the house was cold. I sat on my bed and wrapped myself in Gramma's quilt to keep warm.

I grabbed my notebook and figured I'd work on the next assignment for Verla's class. *Write something that's true,* she had said.

She had given us a list of ideas, in case we got stumped for something to write about. The first thing on the list was this: *Consider your emotional response to a situation. How do you feel? Write it down. What does this feeling make you think of? Where does this emotion take you? Tell the truth.*

Verla said *tell the truth* like it was no big deal. Like I knew what the truth was.

The truth was this: the house felt empty.

I imagined my mom layering the lasagna noodles in the pan—layer of noodles, layer of sauce, layer of noodles, layer of sauce. I imagined her washing the pots in which she had cooked the sauce and noodles, scrubbing them clean and putting them in the drainer.

Before Fox's mother had left, she had washed all the dishes and put them away. That's what Fox had said. The dish drainer was empty; the kitchen was clean.

The dish drainer in our kitchen held the pot from the lasagna noodles and some silverware. The truth was this: I was glad that my mom hadn't put away the pots.

I wrote in my notebook: *I feel empty, like this house.*

It was weird. If my mom had been home, she would have made us all sit down and eat dinner together. She would have asked me a bunch of annoying questions. I would have probably said something mean, and I would have wished I could just go to my room and close the door. But because she wasn't here, I missed her. *I feel lonely,* I wrote. And then, telling the truth, I wrote, *I feel abandoned.*

My dad used to subscribe to *National Geographic* magazine. I remember this article I read in the magazine back when my fourth-grade class was learning about the South Pole. It was all about emperor penguins. They look like roly-poly, happy-go-lucky birds, all dressed up in black and white. But that's not the way it is at all.

Every year, in the dead of winter, these penguins trudge inland over the ice to the place where they lay their eggs. The temperature drops to minus 100 degrees Fahrenheit, and the wind blows so it seems even colder.

For some reason, maybe because the house was cold, I was thinking about those emperor penguins. Verla had said we could write about anything as long as it was true. So I wrote some stuff I remembered from the article: *The emperor penguin lays her egg on the ice. The male penguin rolls the egg up onto his feet and covers it with a big flap of skin on his belly to keep it warm. Then the female penguin leaves, trudging back to the ocean to fish.*

In the article, there had been a photograph of the penguins marching over the ice and snow, a long line of black-and-white birds heading into a white world of nothing. The photographer had been far away and above the penguins—in a helicopter, maybe. Great mountains of blue-white ice—icebergs that had frozen into the pack ice—rose from the field of white.

I wrote: *For two months, the male penguin stands there with the egg on his feet. He can't leave. For two months, he doesn't eat. He huddles with a bunch of other male penguins, trying to stay*

THE WILD GIRLS ✦ 183

warm and keeping that egg warm. That's all he does.

Then the egg hatches. The chick is a ball of gray fluff, with a black head. That's when the female gets back from the ocean.

The next part seemed pretty strange to me when I read about it. This male penguin has been standing around for two months, waiting for the female to get back. He weighs about half what he did when he walked inland. The female is fat and he is thin. And there's this chick, their child, hungry and in need of constant care.

I wrote: *What would you say to someone who took off for two months, leaving you in the snow with an egg on your feet? You probably thought she was never coming back. Maybe you thought she'd been eaten by a killer whale or something.*

The chick that has been standing on top of Dad's feet for all this time has to climb off Dad's feet and step up onto Mom's. How strange that must be. I mean there you are, standing on Dad's feet covered by his belly skin. Then Dad lifts his belly out of the way and nudges you out into the world. A blast of cold air and this mom you don't even know is nudging you to climb up on her feet. What do you say to this mom who has been gone for such a long time?

I stopped writing and read that last sentence over again. As I read it, I realized what I was writing about. *Sometimes it sneaks up on you,* Verla had said. *You're writing about one thing and you realize that you're really writing about something else. Just relax and let it happen.*

I wrote: *I wonder what Fox is doing right now. She's no penguin chick, but it's still very strange to have your mom disappear and then come back. What can she say to this mom who has been gone?*

I curled up under Gramma's quilt, thinking about those penguins, and thinking about Fox. I must have fallen asleep.

The next thing I knew, I heard a soft knock at my door, and my mom stuck her head in. The hallway behind her was dark.

"Hey," she said softly. "I saw your light on."

I blinked at her sleepily as she came into my room and sat down in the rocking chair by the bed. She was wearing jeans that had grass stains on the knees and an old faded T-shirt.

"How are you doing?" she asked.

My mom was rocking in the chair, watching me. It was strange to have her sitting by my bed like that. When I was little, she used to sit by my bed and read to me every night before I went to sleep. Even when I was old enough to read myself, she would read to me. I liked falling asleep to the soft sound of her voice.

It was weird to remember that. I hadn't thought about it for a long time.

"Something happened today," I said. I realized that my eyes were smarting and my breath was catching in my throat. For some reason I didn't really understand, I felt like crying.

Then my mom was sitting on the bed beside me with her arm around my shoulders. "Hey, sweetie, what's the matter?"

I was scared, and I didn't know exactly what I was

scared of. "Gus got a letter from Fox's mom. She ran away five years ago, and now she's back."

I didn't know exactly what I was crying about. It seemed like a good thing that Fox's mom was back, so I shouldn't have been crying about that.

My mom rubbed my back and grabbed me a tissue from the box on the nightstand. "It's okay," she said, even though she didn't know what I was crying about. "Everything will be okay."

I blew my nose in the tissue. "I don't know why I'm crying," I blubbered, but I didn't stop.

"It's okay," she said again. "It must be hard on Fox. You're a good friend to help her out." She rubbed my back, not saying anything for a minute.

Gradually, the tears slowed down a little, and I could breathe. "I came home," I managed to say. "I came home and you weren't here."

"I was at class," she said. "I didn't think . . . you're so independent now. I'm sorry." Her words came out in a rush.

"Fox came home once, and her mother was gone and she never came back." My throat was tight, and I could barely get the words out.

"Oh, sweetie!" My mom hugged me the way she used to hug me when I was little. I usually didn't let her hug me like that anymore, but just this once, I did. She smelled of gardening and sweat. She smelled like my mom. "That isn't ever going to happen to you. You know that, don't you?"

"You and Dad," I said, "I know you're going to a marriage counselor."

My mom nodded. "That's right. I told your father we had to do something."

"Dad thinks going to a counselor is stupid," I said. "I heard him say that."

My mom nodded again. Her lips were pressed together in a thin line. "Your father thinks a lot of things are stupid," she said.

I nodded. "I know."

"I don't know what's going to happen with that," she said. I knew "that" meant everything to do with Dad and the counselor. "But I want you to know that I'm not going anywhere."

I nodded. "Okay," I said.

"I love you, sweetie. You know that, don't you?"

I curled up under Gramma's quilt, feeling a little better.

13

SOMETHING TRUE

The next morning, I went over to Fox's. Fox was in the clearing in the orchard. She had a heap of rocks at her side and she was throwing them overhand at a tree that was about twenty feet away. She had a good aim. When a rock hit the tree, it made a solid *thwack*!

"What's going on?" I asked, stepping around behind her so I wouldn't get hit by a stray rock.

"I'm throwing rocks at a tree." She threw another rock.

"I can see that."

"Then why did you ask?"

I didn't say anything. I just waited, figuring she'd tell me more eventually.

"My dad called my mom last night," she said, and then threw another rock. *Thwack!*

"Yeah?"

"Yeah. I talked with her some. She said she was sorry." *Thwack!*

"She said she was sorry when we talked to her yesterday."

"Yeah. Well, she said it some more. She's really very sorry." *Thwack!* "A lot of nothing."

"Did your dad talk to her?"

"Yeah."

"What did he say?"

"He didn't say much. He mostly listened. I'm sick of the whole thing." Fox threw her last rock and then flopped down in the armchair. "What do you want to do?"

I sat on the ground with my back against the walnut tree. It was a clear, hot summer day. The air was warm and blackbirds were singing in the walnut trees. "We could work on the tree house," I suggested. We had started but hadn't gotten very far.

Fox shook her head.

"We could go down to the creek. Or go through the culvert."

Fox shook her head again. All those things had been fine before, but nothing seemed right, now that Fox's mother had called.

"What do you want to do?" I asked her.

"I could write something for class. We're supposed to write about something true," she said. "Have you written anything yet?"

I told her about the penguins.

"Wow!" she said. "I'm surprised those boy penguins don't just waddle back to the water."

"They can't leave the eggs," I said.

She wasn't listening. She was staring into space. "I could write about my mom, I guess."

"What would you write?"

"I was remembering what it was like when I was little. Some days, she would drink and get headaches and sit in the dark, and I would have to tiptoe around, being really quiet. And sometimes, we'd go to the park, and we would walk and walk. And then sometimes she'd be really happy, and she'd play music by tapping on pots when she was cooking dinner." Fox had tipped her head back. She was looking up at the sky through the leaves of the tree. "That's what I remember."

"You could write about that," I said.

She shook her head. "I don't want to write about that. How come she had to leave, anyway?"

"Do you think it would have been better if she'd stayed?" I asked. "You said your mom and dad were fighting a lot." I couldn't help thinking about that. If your parents fought a lot, was it better if they just got divorced and got it over with? I didn't know.

"I think it would have been better if they never got married."

"Then you wouldn't be here," I pointed out. "That seems like a problem."

"Let's go down to the creek," Fox said.

I followed her through the orchard to the creek. We sat on the muddy bank in the shade of a walnut tree, our bare feet dangling in the cool water. In the summer heat, the creek had almost dried up. But here, a deep pool of water was caught. Water striders, those long-legged insects that skated over the water's surface, skimmed across the pool, each kick of their legs sending out ripples.

A few days before, we had gathered colorful pebbles from the creek bed and stacked them on the bank. In the water, the rocks had looked bright and shiny. Now dry, they were dull—a deep, rich green stone had become a dusty green-gray; a blood-red pebble had faded to the color of mud. "My brother got a rock tumbler for Christmas a couple of years ago," I said. "Maybe we could tumble these rocks to polish them." I thought that idea might distract her.

It didn't work. She was glaring at the water, her mouth set in a grim line.

I took one of the pebbles and tossed it into the still pool. It splashed into the water, its point of impact becoming the center of a circular pattern of spreading ripples.

"I'm glad your parents got married. I'd have died of boredom in Mrs. Parsons's class if you hadn't been there last year."

Fox shook her head, still frowning at the water. "I think my mom asked my dad for a divorce when they were talking last night," she said. "I think she wants to marry someone up in Oregon, and so she wants to get divorced." Fox looked like she was just about to cry.

I handed her a rock. "I bet you can't hit that tree over

there," I said, pointing to a tree across the creek.

She missed with the first ten rocks, but eventually, she nailed it.

* * *

After dinner that night, I went to my room and sat on my bed. I wanted to write in my notebook about hanging out with Fox and talking about her mother, but it wasn't easy to do.

I pulled Gramma's quilt around me.

My grandmother, my mother's mother, had made that quilt. She had pieced it together from fabric that was all different shades of blue and violet. When she gave it to me, she said that some quilts had names. She called this one "Feeling Blue." *It's a crazy quilt, a quilt put together without a lot of rules*, she'd told me.

Gramma told me where some of the pieces of cloth came from. A pale-blue cotton square with daisies on it was from her favorite old sundress. A blue-and-white-checked square of cotton came from an old shirt of Granddad's. Some squares of deep-blue velvet were from the dress my mom wore to a fancy dance in high school.

That had been strange to think about. Those pieces of cloth were from a dress my mom had worn before I existed.

It's all about your family, Gramma had told me when she gave me the quilt. *Bits and pieces of their lives, all sewn together in scraps and patches.*

Write something true, Verla had said, as if that were an easy thing to do.

If you had asked me a few months ago, I would have told you that I didn't like my family much. Now I wrote: *My grandmother made a crazy quilt that she says is about my family. It's bits and pieces, all sewn together.* Then I wrote: *What happens if you cut a piece out? Does the rest unravel?*

I smoothed a blue velvet square and thought about my mom in high school. Her dress was royal blue, my favorite color.

I wrote: *Fox's mother wants a divorce. She's divorcing Gus. Does that mean she's divorcing Fox, too?*

My mom tapped on the door, opened it, and stuck her head in before I had a chance to say, "Come in." There are times when that would have annoyed me, but I was glad to see her.

"I just wanted to see how you were doing," my mom said.

"I'm okay," I said. "What's your favorite color?"

She looked surprised, but she came in and sat on the edge of the bed. "Blue," she said.

"What kind of blue?"

She pointed to one of the velvet squares on the quilt. "That color blue."

I nodded. "That's what I thought."

"Why did you want to know?"

"That's my favorite color, too." I hesitated, and then went on. "I guess I was wondering if Fox and her mother had the same favorite color."

"How's Fox?" my mom asked.

"Her mom wants to divorce Gus."

My mom bit her lip, looking pained.

"So how come people get married, anyway?" I asked her.

"Because they love each other," she said.

"How come they get divorced?"

"People change," she said.

"They don't love each other anymore?"

She frowned down at her hands. "Maybe they still love each other, but they can't live together. Maybe they never really loved each other in the first place. Maybe they just don't fit together the way they used to. I don't know. It's not simple."

Fox had said: *It was a lot simpler when my mother was an enchanted fox.*

I had to agree. "Yeah. It's not simple at all."

"What are you writing?" my mother asked me.

"I'm supposed to be writing something true," I told her. "But it isn't easy."

"Something true about what?"

"About Gramma's quilt," I said.

"That's a good thing to write about," she said.

"Gramma told me that this velvet came from your old dress. She told me that this"—I pointed to a cream-colored square of flannel that was striped with lines of baby blue—"this came from my baby blanket."

My mother nodded.

"Do any of these squares have something to do with Mark?" I asked.

My mother tapped on a pale-blue denim square. "His favorite rompers when he was three," she said.

"What about Dad?" I asked. "Is there anything from him?"

My mom studied the quilt, and then pointed to a strip of dark-blue silk that sliced through the center of the quilt. It cut across all the other squares—a different shape from everything else. It was almost the same color as the velvet from my mother's dress. "An old tie," my mom said. "When Gramma asked for something blue, he laughed. Then he gave that to her. It was his favorite tie before he got a gravy stain on it."

"Why did he laugh?"

"I think that he was happy to be asked. Gramma had been pestering everyone for a piece of fabric. But she hadn't pestered him much." My mom looked down at the quilt, her lips pressed tightly together. "Your dad can be a difficult man to pester. But maybe he felt left out. Maybe he was just happy to be asked." Then she said, "That was a long time ago."

After my mom left, I wrote in my notebook that I didn't know what the truth was. All I could do was write bits and pieces, scraps of conversation, fragments of description. Like the pieces of the quilt—a little bit of this and a little bit of that. In the quilt, all the pieces of cloth added up to something wonderful. But in my notebook, I didn't know what the pieces would add up to.

"Why do people get married, anyway?" Verla said, reading aloud. "It seems kind of stupid, since lots of them get divorced."

I looked at Fox, wondering if Verla was reading her story, but she looked back at me, frowned, and shook her head. I looked around the classroom, trying to figure out who could have written it.

Not Zoom—her ears weren't turning red. Not Bodie—he was listening too closely for that. When Verla read his stuff, he looked at the ceiling and pretended he wasn't interested.

I noticed that Al was chewing on his lip and looking uncomfortable. It was his, I figured.

It wasn't really much of a story. It was all bits and pieces, like what I had written about Gramma's quilt.

"The truth is—people are stupid sometimes. They get married and they have kids," Verla read. "And then they start fighting. Maybe they just shouldn't have kids."

At lunchtime, Bodie, Fox, Zoom, Al, and I all walked to Sproul Plaza. After Verla finished reading Al's story, she asked if anyone had any comments. No one raised a hand.

I walked beside Al for a while, not saying anything. Then I told him, "I asked my mom the same question last night: Why do people get married?"

"Yeah? What did she say?" Al asked.

"She said it wasn't simple."

Al was looking at the ground as he walked. He was a

tall kid. He kept his hands in his pockets and he slouched. "Why did you ask her?"

I scuffed my feet on the ground, thinking about the question. "She and my dad are going to a marriage counselor," I said. "They fight a lot."

Al nodded, still looking at the ground. "My parents used to fight a lot. Then they went to a marriage counselor for a while."

"Did it do any good?" I asked.

He shrugged. "Some, I guess. They kept fighting, but they didn't yell as much. So that was a little better." He glanced sideways at me. "Then they got divorced."

We walked along without talking for a bit. It was a warm, sunny day, but I felt cold.

"You know, there's nothing you can do about it," he told me. "It's all about them; it's not about you. My parents made me go to a counselor, and that's what she told me."

"Well, sometimes they're yelling about me," I said.

"They have to yell about something. Really, they're just yelling because they're mad at each other. All you can do is stay out of the way."

I nodded. "That's what I do."

"If they get divorced, it's not all bad. My dad got me a new terrarium for Mr. Squeeze because he felt bad."

"I don't think my dad would feel bad," I said.

14

THROWN TO THE WOLVES

The next day started out with shouting.

My father was shouting about how he couldn't get any sleep with all the goddamn racket. I heard him stomping around and complaining loudly about the stupid SOB with the noisy truck and about all the noise Mark had made dragging the newspapers around.

I pulled the pillow over my head and tried to go back to sleep. I couldn't. I listened to my father yelling and stomping around. I waited until everything quieted down. Then I got dressed and went to the kitchen.

My mom was sitting at the kitchen table, having a cup of coffee and reading the gardening section of the newspaper. She looked tired.

"Do you want some toast?" I asked her. "I'm going to make some toast."

She looked a little surprised. "Okay," she said.

I made toast with butter for her and for me; poured myself some orange juice; brought it all to the table, and sat down across from her. She wasn't all cheery, like she usually was in the morning.

"What was Dad so mad about?" I asked.

My mom sipped her coffee. I waited for her to laugh and pretend nothing had happened. But she didn't. "There's a new guy delivering newspapers to Mark," she said. "He has a noisy truck."

Three times a week, early in the morning, someone delivered a couple of bundles of newspapers for Mark, leaving them on our front porch. Mark rolled each newspaper, put a rubber band around it, and then rode his bike around the neighborhood, delivering them.

I frowned. "Yeah? So he has a noisy truck."

"The noise woke your father up half an hour before he usually gets up," she said. "He wasn't happy about it."

"So he shouted and woke everybody else up," I said. "Then he went to work."

"That's right."

I thought about that for a minute. "Dad wanted Mark to get a job, right?" I asked.

My mom nodded.

"Now he's unhappy about the job," I said.

"Your father isn't a very happy person."

She wasn't smiling and pretending everything was all right. I wondered if that was the marriage counselor's idea. *Tell the truth,* Verla had said. But I wasn't so sure this was an improvement.

I nibbled on a corner of a piece of toast. I wasn't really hungry.

"If Mark quit, Dad would give him a hard time," I said.

My mom nodded wearily.

"Dad was complaining about money, but he didn't want the money I tried to give him," I said.

She nodded again.

Ask questions, Verla had told us. "Do you know why?" I asked.

She shook her head slowly. "No," she said. "I can't explain it."

"Gus says that sometimes when people fight about money, they aren't really fighting about money."

"Yeah?"

"Yeah. He says that sometimes fighting about money is fighting about power."

She nodded again. "Gus is a smart man." She set down her coffee cup and looked out the window. "Looks like a nice day for gardening," she said.

I knew she was done answering questions. So I drank my orange juice, ate my toast, and put my glass and my plate in the dishwasher. Then I headed for Fox's. I figured I didn't want to be around when Mark came back from his deliveries. I guessed that Mark wouldn't be in a good mood.

Fox was in the clearing in the orchard, but she wasn't in a good mood, either. She was throwing rocks at a tree again.

"What are you doing?" I asked, flopping down in the old armchair.

She gave me an evil look. "Throwing rocks at a tree."

"You did that yesterday."

"Well, I'm doing it again today." She threw another rock. *Thwack!* I was glad I wasn't that tree. "I talked to my mom last night. She and my dad are definitely getting a divorce."

"Maybe that's good," I said. I was trying to be reasonable. "I mean, you don't want her to come back, do you?"

"I don't know," Fox said. "I just wish she hadn't started all this." *Thwack! Thwack! Thwack!* Fox threw three rocks in rapid succession and then picked up the last rock in her pile. "She said she was going to come and visit us." Fox threw the last rock and missed the tree. "I don't want to see her. I don't want to talk about her. I don't want to talk about that stupid fox, either."

"What *do* you want to do?"

"Throw rocks at this tree and work on a story."

I nodded. Verla had told us once that you could work on a story while you were doing dishes or going for a walk or cleaning your room. In fact, she said those were great times to work on a story. *You can work on a story while you're doing anything that doesn't engage your whole attention,* she had said.

"What's the story about?" I asked.

"About a girl who throws rocks," she said. She was glaring at me now. "Maybe she throws rocks at foxes.

Maybe she throws rocks at people who ask her too many questions. Anyway, I'm going to be busy, that's all. I'm working on a story." She threw the last rock. *Thwack*! "I can't hang out with you all the time."

"Okay," I said. "I'll give you a call later."

"Whatever," Fox said, and she threw another rock at the tree. "Just leave me alone."

I went home. My mom was in the kitchen, unloading the dishwasher. She glanced at me as I came in the door. "I thought you were going to Sarah's house," she said.

I shrugged. "She's busy today."

My mom stopped what she was doing. "Yeah? What's going on?"

"She was throwing rocks at a tree. She said she couldn't hang out with me all the time. She was really mad."

My mom was quiet for a minute. She poured herself a cup of coffee and sat down at the kitchen table. "I guess Fox is having a hard time right now."

"I guess so. Her mom and dad are getting divorced."

"Sometimes, when you're having a hard time, you get mad at the wrong people. You understand that, don't you?"

"Yeah," I said, thinking about how mad I'd been at my mom right after we moved. I wasn't mad at her anymore. "Fox must be awfully mad at her mother. She was gone for a long time. But I don't know why she's mad at me."

"If you care about someone, you take care of them even when they're mad at you," my mom said. "Besides, I'll bet she won't be mad tomorrow."

"Maybe," I said, wondering what I was going to do in the meantime.

The doorbell rang.

"That's Mrs. Gordon," my mom said. The Gordons had returned from their vacation in Hawaii.

Mrs. Gordon was talking as soon as she came in the door. She kept talking as my mom poured her a cup of coffee. "I really hope you can lend me a hand," she was saying. "I've got the listing for the Robinsons' house, but the place has zero curb appeal. It's a great house on the inside, but outside it's completely blah. All that lawn and nothing else."

Mrs. Gordon was always talking about curb appeal, which has to do with how nice a house looks when you drive by. To hear her talk about it, curb appeal was really important when you wanted to sell a house.

"So I need your help to dress the yard up a bit," Mrs. Gordon said. "With that class you've been taking in landscape design, I know you'll have some wonderful ideas."

My mom laughed. "I just started taking this class."

Mrs. Gordon waved a hand dismissively. "You had tons of ideas before you took that class. I just want you to take a look and give me some advice and a helping hand."

My mom nodded slowly. "I could take a look."

"Could we do it today?" Mrs. Gordon said. "I've got an appointment with some very motivated buyers tomorrow. I just hate to show it the way it is."

My mom looked at me thoughtfully. "Maybe," she said. "If we can enlist some help."

Mrs. Gordon smiled at me. She was okay, even though she was always in a hurry. "I bet Cindy would join us," she said. "As long as we go out for lunch and get ice-cream sundaes for dessert."

"What do you think?" my mom asked me.

Ice cream sounded good. I was curious about what my mom had been doing in that class of hers. And I didn't have anything else to do. "Sure. If Cindy's going, I'll go." I hadn't seen Cindy since the beginning of the summer.

We went to the Gordons' and got Cindy, and then we all piled into Mrs. Gordon's car.

On the way to the Robinsons' house, Cindy told me about her vacation in Hawaii. Her family had stayed in a condominium near the beach. They went swimming every day. Hawaii sounded pretty, but kind of boring.

The Robinsons' house was a big beige house on a cul-de-sac called Forest Court. The name of the street didn't make much sense. There were no trees, just enormous empty lawns. The house had a FOR SALE sign in the middle of a giant lawn. Looking at that lawn made me think about how much work it would be to mow all that grass. The Robinsons had moved out a month ago, and the house looked a little lonely and sad.

Mrs. Gordon stopped the car, and we got out and

walked halfway to the front door. "See what I mean?" she said. "Big and boring."

"But this yard has so much potential," my mom said. "Take a look at this month's *Sunset* magazine. They did a makeover of a yard just like this, turning it into a lovely cottage garden."

"Maybe I'll buy a copy of *Sunset* and leave it on the coffee table. But what can we do to help this place out in the short run?"

My mom was turning in circles, looking at the yard and at the house. "Well, we could definitely improve that entryway," she said. "We could make a hanging garden there." She waved a hand at a wooden beam that ran along the garage wall beside the path to the front door. "And maybe get some big ceramic pots to put on either side of the door. With something tropical in them—maybe scarlet hibiscus? We could put more flowers by the mailbox. It would be better if there were flowerbeds, but if we got a couple of half barrels to use as planter boxes, we could add some color."

She and Mrs. Gordon talked a bit more, waving their hands around and making all kinds of plans. Then we headed for the nursery.

Cindy and I spent an hour wandering around the nursery while our moms gathered plants and pots and put them in a shopping cart. "What have you been doing in that writing class?" she asked.

That was a tough question to answer, but I gave it a

try. I told her about the stilt-walkers and about getting my face painted and about how Verla kind of seemed to know more than she should. I told her about being in a class of "loose nuts," and I told her about the other kids in the class. She wanted to hear about Bodie and Al, and I admitted that they were kind of cute and not nearly as stupid as the boys in our school.

"Your mom is really into this landscape architecture thing," Cindy said. "She and my mom have been talking about how to redesign our backyard after your mom finishes working on yours. Your mom was saying that she might make a business out of this."

I frowned, knowing that my father would not like that at all.

Finally, our moms wheeled the cart to the checkout stand. My mom usually bought small plants for our yard— she said she liked to watch them grow. But Mrs. Gordon was buying lots of big plants and big pots. She put all the pots in the trunk, but all the potted plants went into the backseat with us. We held potted plants on our laps, and the whole car smelled of dirt and flowers.

We went back to the house that Mrs. Gordon was selling, and my mom put us all to work. The big plants were in ugly plastic pots, so we put those inside the fancy ceramic pots that Mrs. Gordon had bought. We arranged this stuff called sphagnum moss around the top of each plastic pot so that you couldn't see the plastic at all. We filled some other big pots with potting soil and planted ferns and flowers. It was a lot of work, but it was kind of fun, too.

Two hours later, we were done. I had to admit—the plants made a big difference. Pots overflowing with ferns hung from the wooden beam beside the path that led to the front door. On either side of the front door were giant ceramic pots filled with hibiscus. The cool blue-green of the big pots contrasted with the bright red of the hibiscus blossoms. The entryway by the front door felt cool and green and welcoming. Out by the mailbox were great tubs of flowers and ferns.

"It's perfect," Mrs. Gordon kept saying. "Just what the house needed."

My mom smiled. "It's too bad we don't have time to do something with the lawn," she said. "A couple of flower-beds would make a big difference."

"I'll tell that to the people who buy it," Mrs. Gordon said. "They'll need a landscaper. Maybe they could hire you."

Then we went to the ice-cream parlor in town, and we all had burgers and ice-cream sundaes for lunch. Mrs. Gordon insisted that it was her treat to thank my mom for all her help. My mom smiled and said that giving advice about gardening was a pleasure and that no thanks were needed.

Mrs. Gordon frowned at her, pretending to be stern. "You've got to start taking your work a little more seriously. As a consultant . . ."

"I'm not a consultant yet," my mom said. "I'm just a student."

Mrs. Gordon waved a hand, dismissing what my mom had said. "You're really good at this. You've got a real eye for design."

After we had lunch, we went back to the Gordons'. Cindy and I went for a swim while our mothers talked about landscaping and real estate. It was relaxing to hang out in the sun with Cindy. It made me feel a little disloyal to Fox, but it was nice to talk to Cindy about books and Hawaii.

We went home at about four o'clock—plenty of time to make dinner. I was sitting in the family room, thinking about writing my assignment for class, when the phone rang. Mom answered it. She was in the kitchen, but I could hear her from the family room.

"What happened?" she said quickly. She sounded upset. "Is he okay?"

I turned so that I could see her over the counter that divided the family room from the kitchen. "I'll come and get him," she said. "The emergency room, you say?"

It was a cop, calling from the emergency room about my brother Mark. My mom went and brought him home. I went with her. She didn't really ask me to go with her, but I figured she needed some help.

Mark was sitting on a chair in the waiting room, and a cop was sitting there with him. He looked kind of small beside the cop. His shirt was torn. He had a cast on one wrist and a big scrape on one cheek that stood out because his face was so pale.

Pay attention, Verla said. *Not just to what happens, but to how you feel about what happens.*

I felt sorry for Mark. My brother was sometimes a jerk, but he looked so miserable and sick, I couldn't help feeling sorry for him. While my mom talked to the cop, Mark just sat there, looking at the cast on his wrist. He wasn't saying anything. The cop told my mom what had happened.

A family had been having a barbeque at a park on the edge of town. "One of the parents called and reported that three minors were drinking at a picnic table," the cop said. "They were worried about the boys."

Apparently the boys had seen the police car coming and had decided to hightail it out of there. Mark and his bike had ended up in the ditch. He had broken his wrist and messed up his bike in the crash. The other two boys managed to get away because the cops stopped to help Mark.

"He doesn't want to rat out his friends," the cop said. "Do you know who they might have been?"

My mom nodded, glaring at Mark. "My guess would be Jerry and Andrew," she said, her face grim. "Is that right, Mark?"

He looked up from his cast, and then nodded reluctantly.

"I'll call their parents," my mom told the cop.

The cop nodded. "I hope they all made it home in one

piece." He was a nice cop, not making a big deal out of it. He was just saying what happened. "There was an empty fifth of vodka on the picnic table when we got there. But I suspect those boys won't be repeating this anytime soon. Your son got pretty sick."

"You can be sure that Mark won't be doing this again," my mom said.

"I've got his bike in the patrol car," the cop said. "The wheels are bent, but I'd guess the frame can be salvaged."

We loaded the bike in the back of the car. The front wheel was twisted and crazy-looking. It wasn't until we were on our way home that my mom said anything to Mark.

"How could you do something so stupid?" she asked, her voice tight.

"It wasn't my idea," Mark said. "It was Jerry's idea. I just . . ."

"You just went along with him," my mom said. "And then when things got bad, you figured you'd run away."

"We didn't want the cops to catch us," he said. "I knew that Dad would be mad, and—"

"So you decided to make it worse," she said. "You're right. Dad will be angry."

Oh, there was no question of that. My father was angry in the worst sort of way. He was angry and self-righteous, as if this action of Mark's had proven what he thought all along. He yelled at Mark, and Mark just sat there, not making any smart remarks, just looking sad and sick. My father wanted him to keep sitting there while we ate dinner, but Mom insisted that Mark go to his room and go to bed. I didn't eat much myself. I excused myself as soon as I could, leaving my parents to argue.

I tapped on Mark's door. I didn't hear anything, so I opened it. He was lying on the bed, turned toward the wall. "Hey," I said. "I thought I'd see if you needed anything."

I figured he'd tell me to bug off, but I had to ask.

He didn't say anything for a minute. He didn't move. Then he sat up, looking miserable. "Did Mom call Jerry, and Andrew's parents?"

"Yeah. As soon as she could."

I had listened to her end of the conversation, and I knew that Jerry and Andrew were in big trouble.

"They're going to be so mad at me."

"Why?"

"For ratting them out."

"What?" I was shocked. That was so unfair. "You didn't tell Mom anything. She figured it out. And you didn't rat those creeps out to the cop. Besides, *you* should be mad at *them*."

"Yeah? Why?"

How could my own brother be so stupid? "They left you in the ditch and saved their own butts. They threw you to the wolves."

"I was so sick," Mark said.

"Yeah? What was it like?" I'd never been drunk.

"At first it was kind of fun. Then all of a sudden, I couldn't stand up straight. And everything was going around and around." He shuddered, shaking his head. "I don't see how Dad drinks that stuff."

＊　＊　＊

Later on, I was in my room, trying not to listen to my parents argue, even though I could hear their voices through the wall. I heard the phone ring, and my mom called for me to come and get it, grateful for the interruption, I think.

It was Fox. "Hey," she said. "How are you doing?"

"I've been better," I said. I told her all about Mark getting drunk and breaking his wrist. "I'm staying in my room so I don't get caught in the crossfire."

"Wow," she said. "Sounds like a mess. I was calling to apologize for being such a jerk this afternoon. I was really mad at my mom."

"I know. It's okay. Did you write a story?"

"No. I just threw a lot of rocks. So, can you come over tomorrow?"

"Sure."

"You're not mad at me?"

"I'm not mad," I said. And it was true.

Joan cares about her brother.

15

STUPID? NOT STUPID?

That was on Saturday. On Sunday, I went over to Fox's. She wasn't throwing rocks at the tree anymore. She was sitting in the big easy chair and writing in her notebook.

"How are you doing?" she asked.

I shrugged. "My mom and dad argued until really late last night," I told Fox. I had heard them as I tried to go to sleep, a rumbling of unhappy voices that came through my door. I could hear them even when I put my pillow over my head.

"Yeah? Did your mom throw things?"

I shook my head. I had tried to picture my mom throwing something at my father, but I couldn't even imagine it. My mom didn't throw things.

"Maybe she should," Fox said. "Throwing rocks made me feel a little better."

"At least she yells back now. She didn't used to do that." My mom had stopped saying she was sorry all the time. I think the counselor must have told her to stop apologizing. When my father acted like it was her fault that Mark

doans mom. now she yells

had gotten drunk, she said it wasn't. When my father went on about how Mark needed to get a job, she told him that Mark had a job. "She fights back," I said.

"What does your dad do?"

"He just keeps yelling."

"What's he yelling about?"

I thought about that for a minute. It wasn't as if he yelled about only one thing. "He yells about a lot of stuff, but I guess it all comes down to one thing. He's right, and everyone else is wrong and stupid. The people at work are wrong and stupid, and my mom is wrong and stupid, and Mark is wrong and stupid. I mostly keep my mouth shut so I won't be wrong and stupid."

"You're wrong sometimes," Fox said. "But I know you're not stupid."

"Who are you to judge who's stupid and who's not?" I asked her.

"Well, I'm smart enough not to go around thinking I'm stupid."

"Well, if you were stupid, you probably wouldn't be smart enough to know you were stupid."

Fox gave me a long, level look, and then raised one eyebrow. She had picked up that trick from Bodie. "Do you think I'm stupid?" she asked.

"No."

"All right then," she said. "Neither are you."

"All right then," I said. "But my brother is pretty stupid, sometimes."

Fox nodded. "I know that. I mean—he rode his bike into a ditch."

"That was because he was drunk."

"And was getting drunk a smart thing to do?" she asked.

I shook my head.

"Stupid," we said together. Then we laughed at the same time, and I knew that everything was really okay between us.

"I don't think your mom is stupid, though," Fox said. "I think she's pretty smart."

"I guess so," I said reluctantly. I had been so mad at my mom right after we moved. It had been hard to let go of that. But I had to admit that Fox was right: my mom wasn't stupid. The day before, I had been impressed with how smart she was about making that house look good. "Sometimes she's annoying, though."

"Of course," Fox said. "She thinks she can tell you what to do. And that's sure annoying."

We agreed on that.

✳   ✳   ✳

Dinner at my house that night was grim. Nobody had much to say except "pass the salt." My father had decided that Mark should fix his bike as a penance for getting drunk. My father had tried to oversee the work, but Mark's wrist was in a cast, he wasn't very good with tools, and my father wasn't much better. So both of them were miserable.

My mom told me that Mrs. Gordon had called. The

motivated buyers had made an offer on the house, so that was good. But that was the high point of the evening.

Mark and I left the table as soon as we could. My father was still mad, and my mom wasn't trying to jolly him out of it the way she usually did.

On Monday, my father left on a business trip to Los Angeles. My mom took him to the airport. I was in the kitchen when they left on Monday morning. My father was dressed in a business suit, his suitcase was packed. He would be gone for two nights.

"I hope you can manage to keep it together while I'm gone," my father said to my mom. His tone implied that she couldn't possibly do it.

Then they were out the door, leaving us alone. I heard the car drive away.

I was just about to head for Fox's when Mark came out of his room. "Dad's gone?" he asked.

"He just left," I said.

Mark looked relieved. He was carrying a bag of rubber bands, which he set on the table. He went and got a bundle of newspapers from the porch, carrying it in his right hand. He set them beside a chair. I watched as he used a kitchen knife to cut the string that held them together. Awkwardly, using only his right hand, he rolled one of the newspapers. Then he held it between his thighs and put a rubber band on it. His left hand was useless because of the cast.

My brother hadn't always been a jerk. When I was in

second grade and he was in fifth grade, a fourth-grader had knocked me down in the schoolyard and taken my lunch. My brother had knocked down the fourth-grader. *That's my sister*, he had said. *You leave her alone.*

Back when I was in second grade, he had seemed so big and powerful. Now he just seemed miserable. I watched him roll another newspaper. It would take him all morning to roll the newspapers at the rate he was going.

"Give me some of those," I said. "I can help."

He looked up, startled. Without asking again, I grabbed a stack of newspapers and set them on the table beside me. "I'll need some rubber bands," I said, and he shoved some across the table.

For the next hour, we sat there and rolled newspapers. At first, neither of us said anything. I could hear the mockingbird singing, sitting in its favorite perch on the chimney. Its song echoed through the house.

"Dad still hasn't managed to shoot that bird," Mark said.

"I hid the BB gun," I told him.

Mark grinned. "Cool." Then he said, "Thanks for helping."

"No problem. How does your wrist feel?"

"It hurts like hell when I move it," he said.

"Well, at least the cast looks cool." He had been drawing on the cast with a black marking pen. I could see the outlines of comic-book superheroes on the white plaster. I was impressed with how good they looked.

He glanced at it. "Dad will probably be mad that I drew on it."

I shrugged. "Probably. But he'll be mad no matter what you do, so you might as well draw on your cast if you like."

"So do you think Mom and Dad will get a divorce?"

I rolled another newspaper and snapped a rubber band onto it. "I don't know," I said. "I talked with Mom about the marriage counselor."

"What did she say?"

"She said she didn't know what was going to happen."

"Jerry's mom and dad are divorced," Mark said. "He lives with his dad and sees his mom on weekends."

No way would I want to live with my father. "That sounds awful," I said.

"He says it's not too bad. He says he can get them to give him stuff because they feel guilty."

I nodded. "One of my friends said his dad got him a new terrarium for his boa constrictor because he felt bad about the divorce," I said.

"I don't think Dad would feel bad," Mark said.

I nodded again. "That's what I said."

"I think maybe they should get a divorce." He sounded like he didn't much care, one way or the other. But he was frowning and blinking a little too much.

"I don't know," I said.

"They don't seem to like each other much," he said.

That was true. I finished the last paper and threw it on

the stack. I helped Mark stuff all the newspapers in the canvas sack that he used to carry them. He would have to walk his route, rather than riding his bike. His bike was still a mess, and he couldn't ride and throw papers at the same time with one hand in a cast. But he said he was okay, so I said good-bye and headed to Fox's.

I spent the day hanging out with her. We didn't talk about her mom. We didn't talk about my parents fighting. I was tired of talking about all that, and I got the feeling she was, too. So we talked about the other kids in the writing class and wrote some stuff about the wild girls.

It wasn't until late in the afternoon that she mentioned that she and Gus were going to the county fair the next day. "It's my dad's idea," she said. "You want to come?"

I asked my mom at dinner that night if I could go.

"The county fair? That sounds like a great idea," she said. "I'd like to check out the flower show. And they have lots of rides and exhibitions." She looked at my brother and me. "Why don't we all go?"

I waited for my brother to say something about how he was busy and the county fair was stupid, but he didn't. He just shrugged. "Okay," he said.

So we all went to the fair in my mom's car: Gus and my mom in the front seat, me and Fox and my brother in the back.

We got there at around noon. My mom wanted to wander through the hall of gardening displays and the small livestock pavilion. The flower displays were kind of dull, but the small livestock was cool. The pavilion smelled of cedar chips.

I liked the Japanese quail, tiny round birds that made interesting noises. Fox decided she liked the guinea pigs. There was a hairless guinea pig named Wrinkles, a strange-looking gray animal with wrinkled, hairless skin and big black eyes.

"It looks like some kind of alien," Mark said.

The owner, a teenage girl, was standing nearby. "Actually, he's a mutant," she said, smiling.

"That's cool," Mark said, and she and Mark talked a little about aliens and mutants and found out that they read some of the same comic books. The girl admired the drawings on Mark's cast. I could tell that Mark kind of liked this girl with the weird guinea pig. She let us stroke Wrinkles. It was like petting warm suede. Kind of creepy but kind of cool.

My mom and Gus agreed that they liked the goats, one of which tried to eat Mark's T-shirt. A wildlife rescue group had a display at the back of the hall. A great horned owl blinked at us from a perch in a large cage. The volunteer told us that the owl had been shot with a BB gun, but the vet at the wildlife museum had nursed it back to health.

We watched the pig races and the camel-milking demonstration and the chicken-calling contest. Then we went to the midway, a long row of booths and rides and food vendors. The carousel played a clinky-clanky tune, and people screamed on the rides. The smell of corn dogs, caramel corn, and cotton candy hung in the air.

"You've got to try the garlic fries," Gus told my mom. "Great stuff."

"Try your luck and win a prize," a barker called to us from the ring-toss booth. A long row of booths offered chances to win giant stuffed dogs. I wasn't sure why anyone would want a giant stuffed dog, but you could win one by tossing rings over Coke bottles, by popping balloons with darts, by knocking over a stack of metal milk bottles with a baseball, or by shooting out the star in a target with a BB gun.

We didn't stop at the ring-toss booth, but we did go to a food booth. Mark and Fox and Gus got corn dogs and fries, but I wasn't hungry and my mom said all that stuff was too greasy for her. The booth that sold ride tickets was advertising a special: for one price, you could get a pass for all the rides and ride them as many times as you wanted. Fox said she wanted to ride all the rides in the midway.

Carnival rides had always scared me. All of them seemed to be designed to take you up too high and turn you upside down and shake you around, and all the time you thought you were going to get dropped on your head and die.

But Fox really wanted to go on all the rides. Oh, she was willing to skip the carousel, but she wanted to go on everything else.

"I don't know," I said, looking up at the double Ferris wheel. The double Ferris wheel was two Ferris wheels linked together by a pair of giant metal girders. Each wheel spun around and around. The giant bar that joined them whirled around and around, sending one wheel high into the air, and then the other. Just watching them spin made me a little queasy.

"Verla says you have to try new things," Fox reminded me. "It'll give you something to write about."

She was right about what Verla said. I already had plenty to write about, but Fox was so happy at the thought of going on the double Ferris wheel that I didn't really want to say no. It was like the time we walked all the way to the other end of the culvert. It was a challenge, an adventure.

But eating a corn dog before going on a bunch of rides seemed like a bad idea.

We agreed to meet my mom, Mark, and Gus back at the corn-dog booth after an hour. Then we got started.

We went on Tilt-A-Whirl, where we sat in a car that spun around and around as it followed a rolling tilted track. That was okay. Then we rode the Rock-O-Plane, which was kind of a Ferris wheel, only you ride in a little cage that you can rock so it flips upside down.

"Let's see if we can make it flip over," Fox said.

Try new things, I thought as we rocked the cage. We managed to flip over once, and it wasn't nearly as bad as I thought it would be. The ride didn't drop us on our heads, and I felt incredibly strong and brave. "Let's do it again," I said.

We kept rocking the cage, and we figured out that we could get the cage to flip over if we rocked forward right when the cage reached the top of the wheel. We had just figured that out when the ride ended, so we rode it again and managed to flip the car over every time we went over the top. That was cool.

When we got off the ride after our second time, Mark was standing nearby, watching us. "Was that you guys flipping over and over?" he asked.

"It sure was," I said.

He looked at me as if he didn't recognize me. A few years ago, I had refused to ride on a Ferris wheel at a fair in Connecticut because I thought it was too scary. "You've gone nuts," he said.

"That's right." I grinned and turned to Fox. "Want to do it again?"

She did and we did and I felt crazy and powerful, like nothing could hurt me.

"Okay, time for the double Ferris wheel," Fox said.

Anything that doesn't kill you makes you stronger. And later on you can use it in some story. That's what Verla had told us. Standing in line and looking up at the double Ferris wheel, I tried to cling to that thought and to the feeling of crazy power.

Fox knew I was thinking about chickening out, though she didn't admit it. Instead, she started talking. "I remember my mom took me on a Ferris wheel when I was six years old," she told me. "I was scared, but she told me that it was like flying. Haven't you always wanted to fly?"

I nodded reluctantly.

"It's just like flying."

When it was our turn, Fox grabbed my hand and dragged me to the seat. A bored-looking teenager lowered the safety bar across our laps and pushed a lever that started the wheel spinning and sent our car upward.

The seat was rocking gently. I gripped the safety bar. We were looking over the heads of the crowd.

"It's like flying in a rocking chair," Fox said. She wasn't even holding on to the safety bar. She had one hand draped over the back of the seat, the other in her lap. Maybe she was showing off a bit, but she looked completely relaxed. The wheel jerked and we moved upward again. I looked down at the ground.

"Don't look at the ground," Fox said. "Birds don't look at the ground when they fly. They look out into the distance. That's what my mom told me."

I took a deep breath and looked out into the distance. Across the midway, I saw the Rock-O-Plane. It was spinning, and cages were flipping over. This was easy compared to that, I told myself, and I made myself let go of the safety bar.

"This is the boring part," Fox said calmly. "It won't get good until after they have everyone on board."

I made a face. I had a bad feeling about what Fox meant by "getting good."

The wheel moved and stopped, moved and stopped

as people boarded the seats below us. I rested one hand lightly on the safety bar, trying to look relaxed. I was still ready to grab it if I needed to. Finally, we reached the top of the wheel.

"Look there," Fox said, pointing. "Can you find your mom's car in the parking lot?"

We could see over the midway, over the pavilions, over the fence that divided the parking lot from the fairgrounds. Lines of cars shimmered in the sun, and I didn't care which one was my mom's. I knew that Fox was trying to distract me.

The wheel began to move again, carrying us downward. Below, I could see two boys getting into the last empty seat. The ride operator latched the safety bar in place, stepped back, and pushed the big lever that controlled the wheel.

The wheel began to move again, but not just the wheel that held our seat. The giant metal girder that joined our wheel to the other wheel began to turn, swiftly carrying our wheel higher. The wind rushed past my face. We were moving upward and rushing forward, and Fox was right. It was like flying. We were high above everything and everyone and it was wonderful and terrifying, but more wonderful than terrifying. We rushed upward and then we were rushing downward, and I could see the people in the midway, hear the barkers shouting, the music of the carousel. Then we were rising again, leaving it all behind as we flew upward.

Fox was grinning, and I knew that I was, too.

The great girder stopped its spinning when we were high above the midway.

"What do you think?" Fox said.

"It's wonderful." I wasn't afraid anymore. Once again, I felt crazy and powerful and brave. I had felt like this when we spotted the light at the end of the culvert, when we had stepped onto the stage with our faces painted with lipstick. I wondered if it would always be like that: first the fear, and then the glory.

We sat on our rocking seat, high above the world. The cars in the parking lot looked like toys. We were all alone at the top of everything. Nothing could touch us here.

"Your mom was right," I told Fox. "It's like flying."

"Yeah," Fox said, and her voice sounded a little funny. I turned to look at her. She was staring off into the distance. "Sometimes she was right."

"You doing okay?" I asked her.

"It's just strange. She's not a fox anymore, but it's not like I have a mom like you do."

I thought about that for a minute. "You can always borrow my mom," I said. "She likes you."

"She does?"

"Sure. She's always asking me about how you're doing."

"Yeah?"

"Yeah. Ever since that picnic at your house, and that time you interviewed her." The seat rocked a little, but that was okay. I wasn't thinking about how high we were above the ground. I was thinking about Fox and my mom. "She's a pretty good mom," I told Fox. "I mean, you've got to watch out. She'll try to tell you what to wear and stuff like that. And that can be annoying. But she's really okay."

Then the giant girder began to spin again, carrying us downward, and the wind was blowing and we were flying again, but this time we were coming in for a landing.

❋   ❋   ❋

We dropped Fox and Gus off at their house, stopped off and bought some pizza for dinner, and pulled into our driveway at a little after six.

My father was in the living room when we walked in. He was home a day early. "I didn't expect you home tonight," my mom said.

"Obviously not," he said, looking up from his book and frowning. "I called this afternoon, but no one was here. My meetings ended early and I decided I should come home."

"We were at the county fair," I said. Mark had already headed to the kitchen with the pizza. I wanted to rush off, too, but it didn't seem fair to leave my mom by herself.

"How nice," my father said in a sarcastic tone. He was looking at my mom. "I guess you were rewarding Mark for his good behavior lately?"

My mom pressed her lips together and looked at me. "Why don't you go set the table for dinner?" she said.

I was happy to leave.

* * *

We had pizza and salad for dinner.

After complaining about the pizza, my father asked me about the fair. I told him about the hairless guinea pig and the goat that tried to eat Mark's shirt. I told him that I had ridden the double Ferris wheel. But it was hard to think of much to say. He nodded when I talked, but he looked really mad.

I was glad when dinner was over. I helped my mom put the dishes in the dishwasher, and then I went to my room to get my notebook. With all that had happened in the last couple of days, I still hadn't written my assignment for Verla.

I thought about staying in my room to write, but I felt restless. I knew if I stayed inside I would hear my parents arguing, and I didn't want to listen to that. I took my notebook and went to the family room. I opened the sliding-glass door onto the patio.

My father was in the kitchen. "Where are you going?" he said. "It's too late to go out."

He was mad, and I could tell he just wanted to yell at someone about something. It didn't really matter who or what.

"I'm going to sit on the patio and write," I said. "I have to finish my homework for tomorrow's class."

"Be sure to close the door. Our electric bill is bad enough without air-conditioning the backyard."

I resisted the urge to tell him that I'd be happy to close

the door, that I always closed the door. But I just nodded and closed the door behind me.

I went to the far end of the patio, where I could sit in a lawn chair and look back at the house. Through the brightly lit kitchen window, I could see my father. He took a clean glass from the dishwasher, then opened the refrigerator and took out the orange juice. He went to the cupboard beside the stove where the liquor was kept and took out the vodka. He mixed a drink: orange juice with vodka.

I don't remember my father ever being really drunk. Not like you see in movies, where people slur their words and can't walk straight. Not like Mark, riding his bike into a ditch. But every night, pretty much, he mixed himself a drink. Always orange juice and vodka. When I was a little kid, I would fall asleep to the sound of my father's spoon tinkling on the sides of the glass as he stirred.

I watched my father put the spoon in the sink. Through the window, I saw my mom step into the kitchen. She was saying something; I could see her mouth moving. When she stopped talking, she was pressing her lips together hard, as if she were trying to keep words from escaping.

I didn't have to hear what they were saying. I knew that they were arguing about something. My father was saying something mean, and my mom was trying to act like he wasn't being mean.

I turned my chair away from the house toward the orchard. The full moon was rising. Over the back fence, I could see the trees of the old orchard, their leaves silver in the moonlight. In the story about the wild girls, the trees of the enchanted forest were sometimes trees and sometimes beautiful nymphs.

I left my chair and went to the back gate. I opened the gate and stood just outside the backyard, looking at the orchard. It was dark among the trees.

I thought about my assignment from Verla. *Choose a character,* she had said. *It could be you. It could be someone else. Think about what this character wants to do. Think about one small step the character could take right now that moves the character toward his or her desire. Then think about the consequences of taking that action. You got all that? Okay—now write a scene in which the character takes that step. Just one scene. A page or two is plenty.*

Think about what your character wants to do. Okay—suppose the character was a girl like me. What did I want to do?

I felt restless and itchy. I felt like I wanted to run; I wanted to hide. I didn't want to be here. I wanted to leave. I wanted to run away from this house—but not just from this house. I wanted to run away from this life. I wanted to run away to the enchanted forest.

Think about one small step the character could take right now that moves the character toward his or her desire. Then think about the consequences of taking that action.

One small step: I thought about running into the dark orchard and leaving the house behind. Maybe I could hitch a ride to the BART station and take BART to San Francisco. From there, I could take a bus somewhere. That was what Fox's mother had done. She had left it all behind. All the arguing and trouble.

Suppose I did that. It wouldn't really change anything. I'd still be me, still be a half-grown girl. I could take BART to San Francisco—but then what?

I thought about what Gus had said when I interviewed him: he couldn't find books that took him to all of the places he wanted to go. To go to those places, he had to write some books himself.

I had to create the world I wanted to live in. To run away from this life, I'd need to turn into someone else. Who could I be?

From the orchard, I heard the chirping of crickets. Then, from the darkness of the trees, I heard the hooting of an owl, a deep questioning: Who? I thought about the owl, hiding in the darkness of the orchard. I remembered the owl at the fair, watching us with its big golden eyes.

What would it feel like to turn into an owl, I wondered. Eyes growing big so I could see in the darkness. Hearing growing so keen I could hear the rustle of a mouse in the leaves. Arms and fingers stretching out into wings that could carry me away. Feet becoming talons that could snatch up a running mouse.

What would it feel like to fly away from people—away from my mother and my father and my brother, always talking and talking about this and that. *Owls don't have words*, I thought, and I liked that idea. *They don't have words. They don't have hands to hold a pen and write.*

I wrote about listening to my parents arguing, always arguing but never coming right out and saying what they were really angry about. I wrote about standing on the patio while the full moon was rising.

I turned into an owl. The moonlight painted my feathers silver. I looked up at the house—a strange place where people lived. I flapped my wings and rose silently into the night air. I soared over the orchard where wild creatures lived. No one would find me there. I would hunt for mice, and when I caught them, I would crunch their bones in my beak and taste their blood.

16

WALKING TALL

Gus called early the next morning. Fox was sick. She'd been sick to her stomach all night—and he hadn't been feeling all that well, either. At about that time, Mark came out of his bedroom, looking a little green. He had been sick to his stomach all night, too.

Gus blamed the corn dogs. "Mild food poisoning," he said.

My mom agreed. "You'll probably all be fine tomorrow."

Mark went back to bed, Fox and Gus stayed home, and my mom and I took BART to Berkeley. We got to class just as Verla was just telling everyone to sit down. I hurried in, waved good-bye to my mom, tossed my paper onto the pile on Verla's desk, and slid into my chair.

"Good morning," Verla was saying. "I'm going to try something new today. Who wants me to read their work? I'm looking for a volunteer."

I looked at Al; I looked at Bodie; I looked at Zoom. Everyone was looking around, probably hoping that some-one else would raise a hand. Then I made the mistake of looking at Verla. When her eyes met mine, she raised one eyebrow just a little, like she was asking me a question without saying a word.

I'd ridden all the rides at the fair. First the fear, and then the glory. I raised my hand, and Verla smiled.

Then she read what I'd written about turning into an owl.

For the first few sentences, I was uncomfortable, aware that everyone was listening carefully. I wondered if any of them had ever thought about running away from home. What were they thinking about me? Then I thought about what Bodie had said: *what people think doesn't change who I am.* I tried to remember that, but I wasn't quite convinced. I didn't want people thinking I was stupid.

In the end, Verla was the one who made me forget about what the other kids were thinking. When she read my words aloud, it didn't sound like she was reading. It was more like she was the person sitting in the backyard, thinking about how unhappy she was, thinking about becoming an owl. When she spoke my words, they sounded right and true.

She smiled as she reached the end, showing her teeth. In her voice, the last words were a snarl. "I will crunch their bones and taste their blood."

The class was quiet for a moment. Then Verla folded her hands on her desk and asked, in a calm voice that was very different from the voice she had used when reading, "What does this character want?"

Everyone sat there without saying anything. It was probably only a minute, but it seemed like forever.

Ketura raised her hand. "She wants to get away from her family and her life. I can see why. I wouldn't want to be around that."

Verla nodded. "So she wants to get away. What else does she want?"

Jose raised his hand. He never said much in class, so I was surprised. Verla called on him. "The character is really mad, but she knows it wouldn't do any good to talk about it. She just wants to go away and kill something."

I blinked, thinking about that. Was I really that mad? I had written that stuff about catching a mouse and crunching the bones because that's what owls did. But maybe I was kind of mad, too.

Jose was still talking. "It's kind of like a comic book I read once—there's this pack of werewolves who don't put up with crap from anyone. Only instead of turning into a wolf, this girl turns into an owl, and she doesn't kill people, she hunts mice. But she's still mad."

Verla nodded again, smiling. "Good call, Jose," she said. "The character is angry, but she's trying to hide that anger. She directs it at mice, rather than other people."

Al and Samantha both raised their hands. Samantha was like Jose—she never said much. Her hair was cut into bangs, and it always looked like she was trying to hide behind them. She didn't smile much, and when she did, she kept her lips closed. I think that was because she didn't want people to see her braces.

"Samantha first, then Al," Verla said.

"I think she's scared, too," Samantha said in a voice so quiet I had to listen really carefully to hear her. "She wants to fly into the woods so that no one can find her."

That was right, I thought. That was what I had imagined when I wrote the story. I would go into the woods, and no one would ever find me except maybe other owls.

"Al?" Verla said. "Do you have something to add?"

"I think she just wants to find a place where she can be happy," he said.

That was true for sure.

"Isn't that true of just about everyone?" Verla said. "Everyone wants to be happy. So do you think this had a happy ending?"

Everybody thought about that. It was strange that no one raised a hand right away. I thought it was obvious that the ending was very happy. She left. She went off on her own. She didn't have to listen to her parents argue anymore. She didn't have to try to make them happy.

Bodie raised his hand at last. "I think it was happy but not completely," he said. "The character is glad to get away, but she hasn't really gotten away. The story isn't over yet. There'll be consequences. I wonder if she'll turn back into a girl when the full moon sets."

"What does everyone else think?"

Some people talked about the problems that the owl would have. Tyler, another kid who usually didn't say much, said that kids would probably shoot at it with BB guns. Jose said that wouldn't matter because you needed a silver bullet to hurt a werewolf and he figured this owl would be the same. So the kid with the BB gun would need silver BBs, and that wasn't likely.

Matthew said that the woods where the owl lived might get taken over by a housing development and then where would the owl go? Zoom said that the girl's parents would go looking for her, and maybe she would feel bad and go home. I didn't think so, but Zoom seemed pretty sure. She'd never met my father. My mom would go looking for me, but my father would probably just be glad the house was quieter.

Ketura said she wondered whether the owl would end up missing her parents, her home, and her comfortable bed. "I don't think she knows what she's in for," Ketura said.

Finally, after everyone else was done, Verla said, "Very powerful work."

Verla never said anything was good or bad—she always just said it was interesting or powerful or thought-provoking or intriguing or something like that. But I could usually tell if she liked something, and I was pretty sure she liked my story. "Let's take a break," she said. "Then we'll come back and talk about another story."

✹　✹　✹

At break, Zoom came up to talk to me. She told me how much she liked the story, and that was nice. Al came up behind her when she was talking and nodded in agreement, and that felt good.

Bodie asked if we wanted to go to Sproul Plaza and get some lunch, so we went. It felt strange that Fox wasn't there, but I felt great. Verla had read my story and had liked it. I kept grinning; I couldn't help myself.

Bodie asked where Fox was, and I told him about the fair and the rides and the food poisoning. "Done in by a corn dog," he said. "What a way to go."

In Sproul Plaza, we split up. Al and Bodie went to the stand that sold burritos; I joined Zoom at the stand that sold sandwiches. We got our sandwiches, and then I spotted Azalea over at the Circus of Chaos table on the far side of the plaza. We went to talk to her.

"Hey, Joan," she said. "Hey, Zoom. Do you want to try getting tall today?"

"What . . . what do you mean?" I asked.

"Do you want to try walking on stilts? I have a pair that would fit you."

Zoom shook her head, but I was tempted. "I don't know how," I said.

"Not yet," Azalea said. "No one ever knows how to do anything until they do it. Want to give it a try?"

I hesitated, thinking about it. "I don't know. I'd probably fall."

Azalea frowned fiercely, shaking her head. "That is

the wrong attitude. That's a Failure of the Imagination."
When she said that, I heard it in capital letters. By her tone,
I knew that a Failure of the Imagination was a terrible and
contemptible thing. "All it takes to walk on stilts is imagination. If you believe that you can walk on stilts, then you
can." She looked at me. "What do you think?"

I looked at Zoom and shrugged. "I guess I could try
walking on stilts."

"You guess you could try?" Azalea made a face. "Pretty wishy-washy."

Bodie had arrived with his burrito. Al was right behind
him. "You can walk on stilts," Bodie said. "It's easy."

"All right," I said. "I can walk on stilts."

"Of course you can," Azalea said. "Let's do it."

Zoom was watching me; her eyes were enormous.

Azalea had me sit on the concrete wall behind the
table. She positioned my sneakers on the stilts and strapped
them in place. Then she strapped the knee brace at the top
of the stilt to my shin just below my knee.

"Perfect," she said. "Now we just have to get you walking. Grab my hands."

I put my hands in hers.

"I'm going to pull you up," she said. "Just relax and
balance."

She pulled on my hands, and suddenly I was standing
high off the ground, balancing on two long sticks. There
was no safety bar to hang on to. I swayed forward, and my

grip on Azalea's hands stopped me from falling. I teetered backward, and she stopped me again. I gripped her hands tightly.

"What do I do if I fall?" I asked. This was crazy. I couldn't even stand on these things, let alone walk.

"You won't fall," she said. "That's an advanced move, and I don't have time to teach you that today. Today, you'll just walk."

"I can't even stand."

"Walking is easier than standing," she said. "Take a step."

"I can't."

"Just lift your knee up and move your foot forward."

She said it so matter-of-factly that I managed to do it. I clung to her hands, and I didn't fall.

"Find your balance point," she said. "Don't look at me. Don't look at the ground. Look off into the distance. Hold your head up high. Look at Jasmine." She jerked her head in the direction of the stilt walker on the other side of the plaza. "That's what you'll look like."

I looked at Jasmine. She was dancing to the drum music, her braided hair swaying in time. She looked beautiful.

"Jasmine just learned to stilt walk a few months ago," Azalea said. "Now move your other foot. Lift your knee. Move where you want, and I'll follow you."

Azalea's hands were always there, right where I needed them.

"You don't need to hold on tight," she said. "Just balance and relax."

Easy for her to say, I thought, but I managed to loosen my grip. I took another step. I could walk, I thought, but only if I held on to her hands.

"That's it," she said. "Just walk. You've been walking for years. All you've done is get a little taller. Stand up straight. Good posture helps. Keep your feet moving. You have to keep walking all the time. Take small steps."

A little taller? I was a lot taller. I could see over Azalea's head. Everyone was shorter than I was. I took another step, still holding her hand.

"Now you need to let go of my hands, and you'll be walking on your own."

I almost said, "I can't," but I stopped myself. *You have to believe*, I thought. *All it takes is imagination. Imagination and balance.*

"I could let go of one hand," I said.

"Great. That's a start."

I let go of one hand. I kept walking, taking small steps. It started to feel okay. I loosened my grip on her other hand.

"Perfect," Azalea said. "You're walking."

I was walking, I thought, and I let go of her hand and took a step. I started to teeter, but Azalea was right there, her hand ready to help. I was walking, taller than anyone. I felt tall and elegant and wonderful.

"That's it," she said. She was still there beside me, but I didn't need her help. I was balanced, and I believed—I knew without a doubt—that I could walk on stilts. I could see over her head. I could see over everyone's heads. It was like being at the top of the double Ferris wheel, only better.

*   *   *

After class, I told my mom about Verla reading my story and about walking on stilts.

"What was your story about?" she asked me.

I didn't know what to say. Before class, I might have been able to say it was about a girl who turned into an owl. But after the class discussion, I knew that it was actually about how mad and scared I was. I didn't really want my mom to know about that. My father was giving her such a hard time—she didn't need to be worrying about me as well.

"It's kind of hard to describe," I said.

"I'd like to read it."

"Okay, I guess," I said reluctantly. Maybe she'd forget about it by the time we got home. I changed the subject. "Walking on stilts was really great."

"Weren't you afraid of falling?" she asked.

"I wasn't allowed to fall," I told her. "Azalea said that falling was an advanced move that she didn't have time to teach me. So she told me I wasn't allowed to fall."

My mom frowned, a little puzzled. "Who's Azalea?"

"She's with the Circus of Chaos. She's the one who painted my face. She says that if you believe you can walk on stilts, you can. And she's right. As soon as I really believed I could do it, I could."

My mom blinked and shook her head. "A stilt walker and a face painter," she said. "That's really interesting. I'd like to meet her."

The funny thing was—she sounded like she meant it.

17

HAVE YOU EVER WANTED TO FLY AWAY?

Verla said that sometimes you should skip over stuff to keep a story interesting. Because some of the stuff that happens is interesting and some is just filler. "No one cares what you had for breakfast," she told the class. "People care when something goes very wrong or when something goes very right. Or when something changes from wrong to right."

So I'm going to skip over some time pretty quickly. Mark and Fox and Gus got better from their food poisoning. Fox and I hung out. My mom asked me for my story again, so I gave it to her, but then she got a phone call from Mrs. Gordon about helping get a house ready to show. I saw her put the story in a stack of papers that she had to read for her landscaping class and then she got distracted. So I thought she wouldn't read it for a while, and that was okay with me.

One strange thing happened, though. One evening, as the sky turned a deep royal blue and the mockingbird perched on the chimney top and sang, I was sitting in the backyard with my notebook, thinking about our next writing assignment.

I was thinking about that when my father came outside and sat in the lawn chair beside me. He was carrying his drink with him.

I waited for him to start grousing about how noisy the mockingbird was, but he didn't.

"You still writing that book?" he asked.

"Yeah."

"You didn't tell me what you're writing about," he said.

"My life," I said.

"How's the writing going?"

"Fine. Right now I'm doing my homework." I figured that would make him leave me alone. But it didn't work.

"What's your homework?"

"We're working on dialogue. I'm supposed to write a scene where two people are arguing."

"I see," he said. "You should be good at that. You've heard enough of it lately."

I didn't say anything. I couldn't think of anything to say that wouldn't get me into trouble. I was surprised he'd even mentioned it.

"Have you started writing the argument?" he asked.

I nodded.

"What are the people arguing about?"

I hesitated, and then said, "About money. At least, that's what they say they're arguing about."

"I guess you've heard a few arguments like that," he said.

"Yeah," I said cautiously, wary of a trap.

"Who's winning?"

I wasn't falling into that trap. "Verla, my teacher, says that we should try to write an argument that no one wins."

"Sounds like it would go on forever," my father said.

I shrugged. An argument only goes on forever if no one gives in or no one walks away. But I didn't say that.

"I guess you know that your mother and I aren't getting along."

I didn't really know what to say. I'd have to be deaf and stupid not to know. "I know you're going to a marriage counselor."

"Some stupid quack," my father said. "That's your mother's idea."

I don't know exactly what happened then. I didn't like the way he said "your mother," as if she had nothing to do with him. I didn't even know the marriage counselor, but I didn't think he was stupid.

"Why do you think everyone is stupid?" The words just popped out of my mouth before I could stop them.

He frowned at me. "What?"

There was no going back. It was sort of like getting on the double Ferris wheel. Once you were in the seat, it was too late to change your mind. "I know you're smart, but that doesn't mean everybody else is stupid," I said. "Mom's not stupid. I'm not stupid."

"I didn't say you were stupid. I didn't say your mother was stupid." His voice was a little louder. He wasn't quite yelling yet.

No, he didn't exactly say she was stupid or that I was stupid, but everything he said pointed in that direction. "You're always saying her ideas are stupid. You said that the writing class was one of her harebrained schemes. You said that going to the counselor is stupid."

"You and your mother both have some stupid ideas," he said. "But . . ."

"That's pretty close to saying we're stupid," I said. "What's the difference?"

He was staring at me. "What's gotten into you, anyway?"

I didn't know what to say for a minute. What had gotten into me? In Verla's class, we had discussions where we pointed out the implications of what a character did. "Subtext," I said.

"What?"

"When you write an argument," I said, "you have to pay attention to subtext. That's what's happening under the surface. Under the surface, you're always saying we're stupid. I don't think I'm stupid. I don't think Mom is stupid."

My father was staring at me.

"I'd better go finish my homework," I said. I grabbed my notebook and left before he could start yelling at me.

The next morning, my mom asked me how I was doing. "Your father said you were upset about the marriage counselor," she said.

I shook my head. "Not really," I said. She waited, and after a minute I went on. "Dad said the marriage counselor was a stupid quack. I told Dad that he acted like everyone was stupid, but everyone wasn't stupid. I told him you weren't stupid."

She blinked, startled. "Well, thank you," she said.

"I'm going to Fox's." I was out the door before she could call me back.

★　★　★

Fox wasn't in the clearing when I got there. I went to the house and climbed the steps to the porch. Through the screen door, I could see into the kitchen. Gus and Fox were sitting at the kitchen table with a man and a woman.

Fox was looking at the woman.

Notice the details, Verla had told us. *It's easy to see what's on the surface. Try to see what's below the surface. Listen to what people are saying, but figure out what they aren't saying. What's the subtext?*

Fox was looking particularly fierce. She was staring at the woman.

The woman looked ordinary enough. She wore a flowered sundress and sandals. She had short, curly, reddish brown hair. She was a little younger than my mom. Her shoulders were hunched forward. Her right hand gripped her left hand, twisting a ring on her finger. She looked uncomfortable.

The man who sat beside her wore a short-sleeved plaid shirt and slacks. He had his arms crossed over his chest. His expression reminded me of my brother when my mom called him away from his comic books and made him sit at the dinner table. He didn't want to be there.

From the porch, I could hear the woman talking. She was saying something about what a nice little house this was. As she spoke, she was looking around the room: at the bookshelves that overflowed with books and papers, at the cracking linoleum on the floor, at the peeling paint, at the clippings and photos stuck to the refrigerator with magnets, at Fox's face. Her eyes were never still.

The woman was nervous, I thought. And she didn't really think it was a nice house. The man was uncomfortable. But who were they and what were they doing here?

"Is that you?" the woman asked. She stood up, walked across the kitchen to the refrigerator, and took a newspaper clipping from under a magnet. I could guess what it was: Gus had put the article about our reading on the refrigerator. She was looking at the photo of Fox and me in our lipstick war paint.

"What's this all about?" she was asking.

I glanced at Fox's face: she looked desperate. She didn't say anything.

"Hello," I called, pushing open the screen door.

Gus introduced me, calling me Joan, instead of Newt. The woman gave me a wide-eyed look. She didn't smile.

"Joan," she said. "We spoke on the phone."

That was when I realized who she was. This was Fox's mother, the woman I had been rude to when she was just a voice on the phone. "Oh, yeah," I said weakly.

"Nita and Joe came to visit," Gus said, as if I couldn't see that.

I shot a desperate look at Fox. She was still sitting at the table, managing to look fierce and miserable at the same time.

"Joan and Sarah won a prize for a story they wrote," Gus was explaining to Fox's mother. "That photo was taken at the ceremony."

"A writing contest?" Fox's mother said. "A sure sign that she takes after you." She turned to Fox. "But why is your face painted?"

She was talking to Fox, but I answered. I figured, given Fox's expression, that she was in no shape to answer.

At least, I tried to answer. I explained that we needed to do it because the story was about wild girls. I told her that we needed to look the part.

She smiled and nodded. But she looked puzzled, even though she was smiling.

Then Fox said, "We're going to go play in the orchard, okay?" And before Gus could say "Okay," she was out of her chair.

"That sounds fine," Gus said as Fox headed for the door. I noticed that Fox's mother looked a little startled and upset, but I didn't stick around to figure out the subtext.

✦   ✦   ✦

"Who's the guy with her?" I asked Fox after we had safely escaped to the clearing in the orchard. She was in the armchair, sitting with her knees bent against her chest, her arms wrapped around her knees. I leaned against the tree. It was great to be outside, out of the kitchen, away from the house and Fox's visitors.

"Her boyfriend, Joe," Fox said. By her tone, Fox didn't think much of Joe. Or of her mother, for that matter.

"She's not like I remembered," Fox said.

"How is she different?" I asked.

"She's just . . ." Fox paused and shook her head, thinking. "She's just not like I remembered. She used to be scary sometimes and fun sometimes. Now she's . . . She seems kind of ordinary, I guess."

I nodded slowly. "You're probably not like she remembers you," I pointed out.

"She's a librarian," Fox said, as if being a librarian were a crime. "She doesn't play music anymore. She told Dad that she had 'cleaned up her act.'"

"There's nothing wrong with being a librarian," I said. "And your dad cleaned up his act, too."

"Yeah, he quit drinking. But he's not boring." Fox shook her head again. She rested her chin on her knees. Her face was all screwed up, and she looked like she might start crying.

"It was easier when she was an enchanted fox," I said.

Fox nodded. "She's sure no enchanted fox," she said

sadly. "I guess I can't be the Queen of the Foxes anymore."

I shook my head. "The way I figure it, you're still the Queen of the Foxes," I said.

She looked at me, blinking a little. "How do you figure that?"

"Well, you said it yourself," I told her. "She's different now."

"Yeah?"

I was thinking hard, trying to figure out a story that would work. *Stories are powerful,* Verla had said. *Stories shape your reality.*

"You figured that she turned into a fox," I said. "But suppose something else happened?"

"Like what?"

I had been leaning forward, but now I leaned back, looking up at the leaves of the walnut tree. I remembered the story she had told me about the woman who became a fox, and I told her this story.

Once there was a woman who did not like who she was. She felt torn in two, like she wanted to go in two different directions, though she couldn't have told you what those directions were. She knew that part of her wanted to run away, and part wanted to stay where she was. She knew that part of her was wild and fearless and threw things, and part of her was scared all the time and wanted to sit in the dark.

She lived with her husband near Golden Gate Park in San

Francisco, and she had a little girl who was just old enough to go to school. One day, when her little girl was at school, she went into Golden Gate Park. It's a big park, even though it's in the middle of the city.

At this point, Fox interrupted. "I told you this story," she said.

"Just wait," I said. "It's not the same story."

Fox made a face, but she stopped talking. I went on.

So the woman went into the park and walked until she was deep in the woods. She left the trail and wandered among the trees.

That was when it started to rain—just a drizzle at first, then big drops of rain that soaked her shirt and jeans. She looked around for somewhere to get out of the rain, and she found a hollow log. She crawled inside the log, where it was warm and dry. She lay there, listening to the rain, and she fell asleep.

When she woke up, she felt strange and confused. She was still a woman, but something was different. She crawled out of the log and looked around. Just a few feet from her, sitting in a patch of sunlight that shone through the trees, was a fox. And she recognized that the fox was part of her.

While she slept, she had split into two parts. There was the woman who was scared and wanted to run away. And there was the fox that was wild and wanted to stay.

So the woman took a bus to Portland and figured out how to live as a woman, with no fox inside of her. And the fox stayed behind to look after the little girl.

"So that's what happened to your mother," I told Fox. "The woman that's in there talking to Gus is the scared part of her, the part that ran away."

"And the rest is the fox," Fox said.

I nodded.

"Okay," Fox said. "I could go along with that." Then she gave me a sideways look. "I don't really believe it, you know. But I could go along with it."

"That's good enough," I said. "You can believe it just as much as you believed she was a fox."

Fox nodded. "That's right. I'll believe it just that much."

"So you know that you are still the Queen of the Foxes," I said.

Fox just smiled.

✦ ✦ ✦

After dinner that evening, I was sitting in my room, writing in my notebook. I was writing down the story I had told Fox when there was a knock at the door.

"Yeah?" I said, hoping it wasn't my dad.

My mom came in. I was glad it wasn't my dad until I noticed that she was holding the story I'd written about the owl.

Describe what you see, Verla said.

My mom was holding my story tightly, as if she didn't want to let it go. She sat down on my bed.

"I read your story. It's a good story," she said, but it didn't sound like she meant it. "When did you write it?"

She was biting her lip; her face was pinched and sad.

"After we went to the carnival," I said. "I was sitting in the backyard, thinking about the owl I saw at the carnival."

"And your father and I were fighting," she said softly.

I nodded.

"That made you want to run away," she said.

"Fly away," I corrected her. "Like an owl in the night."

"I'm sorry," she said. "I'm sorry we're fighting. I'm sorry that makes you want to fly away."

"Are you and Dad still going to marriage counseling?" I asked.

She nodded.

"It doesn't seem like it's doing much good," I said. It was weird to say that. You know that fairy tale, where the little kid says: "Hey, the Emperor has no clothes." It was like that. I was telling her something she already knew.

She nodded again. "Your father doesn't really want to be married."

"So are you getting a divorce?"

She didn't start crying, but she looked like she wanted to. "We're talking about it." She looked at me. "Does that make you want to turn into an owl and fly away?"

I thought about that. It seemed like I should be upset, but I wasn't. My mom was telling me the truth now. I was sure of that. She wasn't pretending that everything was just fine, when it wasn't.

"No," I said slowly. "I want to run away when you fight, when Dad's being mean and you're pretending he isn't, when Dad's making fun of everyone. When Dad is away on a business trip, stuff is much better."

She nodded. "I know what you mean."

Ask questions, Verla said.

"Has he always been like this?" I asked her.

"What do you mean?"

I thought carefully about my words. It was hard to find the right ones. "I don't know. So sarcastic, I guess. So mean to people."

I thought she might say, "You shouldn't say that about your father," but she didn't.

"No," she said slowly. "He hasn't always been like that."

"He's always yelling about something," I said. "He always has to have everything his way."

"He's not a patient man," my mom said. "He's very smart. Smarter than anyone else—and proud of being so smart. I guess he gets more and more impatient with other people who aren't as smart as he is. That's why he gets so mad at me, I think."

I thought about that for a moment. "He's not very smart about people," I said.

My mom nodded. "I suppose you're right."

"*You're* smart about people," I told her.

"I'm glad you think so." She looked down at the story in her hands. It was crumpled where she had gripped it hard. She flattened it out on her knee, trying to smooth it out.

"Have you ever wanted to fly away?" I asked her.

She looked at me thoughtfully. "Not exactly," she said slowly. "When I left home and went to art school, I remember I used to write in my journal. I remember writing once about how learning to paint is like learning to fly. I felt like I could just spread my wings and take off." She was smiling. "I wonder if writing is kind of like that for you."

I nodded. "Yeah. Sometimes."

"That's good."

I nodded again. "You know, I'm not going to run away or anything stupid like that."

"I know that," she said. But I guessed, by the way she smiled when she said it, that she was glad to hear me say so.

18

A Different World

At the next class, Verla talked about conversations and arguments. "Sometimes, I'll have an argument. Then as soon as it's over and the other person isn't there anymore, I'll know exactly what I should have said. Has that ever happened to you?"

Almost everybody nodded.

"The French have a term for that," Verla said. "They call it *esprit d'escalier*, wit of the staircase. It means you think of the perfect witty thing to say when you have left the room and you're on the stairs, heading home." She wrote the French phrase on the board and I copied it into my notebook. "Here's one of the advantages of being a writer," she said. "You can rewrite arguments until they are just right."

I nodded. I already knew that one. The night before, I had rewritten the argument with my father. In my version, he admitted that he was wrong and apologized. That would never happen. But it felt great to write it.

Verla read Samantha's dialogue. It was about a girl

who was a superhero. She was arguing with her mother, who wanted to know why she had been late to school. The girl had been late because she had been stopping a bank robbery, but she couldn't tell her mom that. The girl was really frustrated with her mother's nagging. The story was kind of silly, but pretty good.

After we talked about Samantha's dialogue, Verla gave us our next assignment. "You've all done a great job of writing a conversation, but all of you wrote from a kid's point of view. For next week, I want you to do an exercise in viewpoint. I want you to take the argument that you wrote and write it over again. Only this time, I want you to tell it from the point of view of the other character. Take Samantha's dialogue, for instance. It's told from the girl's point of view. Samantha told us all about what the girl was feeling and thinking. That's great—but now I want Samantha to write it again, only she has to tell it from the mother's point of view. Do you understand?"

I was supposed to write the argument with my father from his point of view. That wasn't going to be easy.

Samantha raised her hand. "But I can't write it from the mom's point of view. I don't know what the mom is thinking."

Verla smiled. "I think you know the answer to that by now."

Samantha frowned. "I guess I should ask my mom," she said. "Or make something up."

"You got it. Either option would work—but you might

learn more by asking. If you don't know, ask a question. Or two. Or six. Or as many as it takes."

I stared at her, trying to imagine asking my dad about how he felt. I couldn't do it.

Verla looked around at the class. "I've told you before that writing is about looking at the world carefully. But that's only part of it. Another part of it is looking at the world from another point of view. It's a different world when you see it through someone else's eyes."

＊ ＊ ＊

Fox and I spent the next day improving our platform in the old walnut tree. We didn't talk about it, but I think we were both avoiding the assignment Verla had given us. We didn't even want to think about it.

So we talked about sleeping out in the orchard—maybe in the tree house if we could make a better platform. I said I'd ask my mom if I could spend the night.

Fox got Gus to consult with us on how to improve our tree house. He looked at the platform we had made by wedging boards between the branches and said that he thought he could give us a better foundation. Then he got some steel cables from the hardware store and some long bolts. He bolted a couple of two-by-fours to the tree's thickest branches, so that we could lay the boards between them.

Then we dragged boards from the lumber pile beside Fox's house and hauled them out to the clearing. We borrowed a saw and a hammer and nails from Gus's toolbox and spent all afternoon sawing boards to the right length and dragging them up into the tree. Fox would climb up the tree, and I would hand her boards from below. She would haul them up and lay them across the structure Gus had built.

It wasn't until late in the afternoon on the second day, when we were nailing the boards into place, that we talked about the assignment.

"I wrote a conversation between the wild girl and her mother," Fox told me. She was hammering a nail into place. *Bang!* "Her mother has turned into a woman again." *Bang!* "The wild girl isn't all that happy about it at all." *Bang!* "I figure I know how the wild girl feels. But I don't know what that fox woman is thinking." *Bang!* She reached for another nail.

"I know what you mean," I said. I was mostly watching and handing Fox nails at that point. "I'm supposed to figure out what my father is thinking." I shook my head. "No way."

Fox hammered another nail into place. *Bang! Bang! Bang!* Then she sat back on her heels. "I guess you could ask him," she said. "I guess he could tell you."

I handed Fox another nail. "Oh, sure," I said in a sarcastic tone. "I'll ask my father. And you could ask your mother how that fox feels. She wouldn't know what you were talking about."

Fox hammered another nail into place. *Bang! Bang! Bang!* "Maybe I will ask my mom," she said. She sat back and stared at the nail she had just smacked into place.

"Okay," I said. "Then I'll ask my father."

It was kind of like agreeing to go on the rides at the fair. It was scary, but not as scary as it would have been without Fox.

✿　✿　✿

That evening, I was sitting on my bed with my notebook in my lap, thinking about talking to my father. I didn't know how to begin. So I worked on rewriting the argument instead.

My father thinks everyone is stupid. When I wrote the argument with my father for our last assignment, that was how I started out:

My father thinks everyone is stupid. He even thinks that the mockingbird that sits on the chimney and sings is stupid. He wants to find the BB gun and kill that bird.

Now I had to write that argument from my father's point of view. I had written the first sentence:

Everyone is stupid. That idiotic bird makes a racket every morning and I can't sleep. I'm going to find the BB gun and kill that bird.

Verla says that no one thinks of himself as a villain. Even the nastiest person thinks that he is in the right. She asked us to keep that in mind when we rewrote our arguments. I didn't know how to do that.

Someone knocked on my door.

"Come on in," I shouted, figuring it was my mom.

It was my father. He came in and closed the door

behind him. "I wanted to talk to you," he said.

I stared at him, wondering whether he was going to yell at me. I didn't say anything, but he came in and sat in the rocking chair by the bed. "Your mother showed me the story you wrote," he said. "The one about the owl."

My father wasn't looking at me. He was looking down at the drink in his hands. It looked like orange juice, but I knew that it was orange juice and vodka. "I was surprised," he said. "But I guess I shouldn't have been."

Ask questions, Verla said. *It's the only way to learn.* "What were you surprised about?"

He looked at me then. "You understand how I feel," he said. "You feel the same way."

I was astonished. "What do you mean?"

"You feel trapped. You feel angry. You want to fly away."

I stared at him.

"I feel the same way," he said.

He felt trapped? He was a grown-up. He could do what he wanted. *Ask questions.* "Why do you feel trapped?"

He frowned. "You told me before that you were learning to ask questions. I didn't realize how troublesome that was going to be."

I shrugged. "It's the only way to learn," I said.

He looked down at his drink again. "You know that your mother and I don't get along. You don't like it when we fight. I don't like it, either. We fight, I drink, I wake up with a headache, and we fight again."

"Are you getting a divorce?" I asked.

He shrugged. "I don't know."

"Do you want to get a divorce?"

"I try to take care of my family," he said. "I earn money to take care of my family. I work hard."

"What do you want?" I asked. *That was the key,* Verla said. What does the character want?

"I want peace and quiet," he said. "I want respect." He shook his head. "And sometimes I want to fly away."

After my father left, I rewrote the argument. I began:

My head aches. There's a bird making a racket on top of the chimney, and it makes my head ache even more. I am angry. I am trapped, and the bird keeps on singing.

Joans dad came
in and talked to
Jaan for the first
time,

19

I Wouldn't Go in There
If I Were You

My mom said I could spend the night at Fox's, and Gus agreed that we could sleep in the tree house. So the next night, I ate dinner at Fox's. Fox and I had gathered big rocks and arranged them around a shallow hole that Gus had dug in the yard near the porch. With Gus's help, we built a fire and let it burn down to coals. Gus showed us how to wrap up pieces of chicken in tinfoil and we cooked them in the coals. Then we roasted marshmallows.

By that time, it was getting dark. The moon was up, and it cast a silvery light over the junk in the yard.

Fox and I took our flashlights and went out to the clearing. Gus went with us and waited while we climbed up into the tree. Fox and I had already put our sleeping bags up in the tree. Gus had rigged a railing around our platform so we wouldn't roll off.

We lay down on the platform, which was just long enough and wide enough for the two of us. I wedged my flashlight between the platform and the tree, right by my hand, in case I needed it in the middle of the night.

"You got everything you need?" he asked.

"We have everything," Fox said confidently. We had water bottles in case we got thirsty and peanut butter and crackers in case we got hungry, and we each had a sleeping bag and a pillow.

"Well, I'll be at the house if you need anything," he said.

"We don't need anything!" Fox said impatiently. "We'll be fine."

Gus finally left. I listened as he walked away, his footsteps loud in the stillness of the night. I could smell the woodsmoke of the campfire. Above me, the leaves of the walnut tree made patterns of darkness against the moonlit sky.

"Isn't this great!" Fox said.

It was great. It was like being in the enchanted forest with the wild girls. Somewhere in the distance, an owl called in the darkness.

"I wonder what that owl is trying to say," I said. "If this were the enchanted forest, we'd know."

"We can always make something up," Fox said.

The owl called in the darkness again, and I told Fox what my dad had said about the story I'd written about changing into an owl. "He said he understood how I felt. He said he wants to fly away, too," I said.

We lay in the darkness, looking up at the leaves and the moonlit sky, thinking about how strange that was.

"I talked to my mom," Fox said. "She called me. My

dad had given her a copy of our story about the wild girls, and she wanted to talk about it."

It seemed so weird. My dad came and talked to me because of a story. Fox's mom called because of a story.

"She wanted to know how I came up with the idea," Fox said. "So I told her about the fox that I saw in the park, after she disappeared."

"What did she say?"

"She was quiet for a while. Then she said, 'The wild girl is friends with the fox. Do you think we could be friends?'"

"What did you say?"

She shrugged. "I said I didn't know. But we kept talking for a while. She said that she wasn't much good as a mom, but she might be better as an enchanted fox. So I said we could try. I talked to my dad about it, and he said he thought it was worth a try."

I nodded. "If you didn't think of her as a mom, it could work."

Fox nodded. "She never was much of a mom anyway. Not like your mom."

I thought about that. "Well, don't forget you can have my mom on loan, whenever you want her."

"Okay, then. I've got an enchanted fox and a mom on loan. That could work."

The owl called in the darkness. It seemed strange that the owls had scared me so much the first time I found my way to Fox's in the dark. That seemed like such a long time ago.

"You know—we only have two more classes with Verla to go," Fox said.

"I know." I had thought about that, but I hadn't said anything. In June, when the class began, it seemed like it would go on forever. Now it was almost over.

It seemed to me that we were just getting started. I had filled the notebook that Gus had given me and half-filled another that I got at the drugstore. I knew that I had a lot more to learn. I didn't want to talk about it.

"If this were the enchanted forest, we'd have mattresses stuffed with straw," I said. The boards were really hard.

"If this were the enchanted forest, the evil king's men would be hunting for us," Fox said.

"If this were the enchanted forest," I murmured, "the nymphs would be singing us to sleep."

Even though the boards were hard and I wished I had a straw mattress, eventually I fell asleep. I woke up suddenly when Fox poked me in the ribs. "Shhh," she whispered. "Look down there."

The moon was low in the sky but still bright. Down in the clearing below, I could see the armchair and the flat boulder in front of it. I saw something move in the shadow of the boulder. "What . . . ?" I started to whisper, but Fox nudged me again.

Then a fox jumped up on the boulder. As I watched the fox sniff the boulder (where Fox and I had eaten peanut butter and crackers for lunch), another fox jumped up.

One more fox, bigger than the first two, was sitting on the seat of the armchair, watching the smaller foxes on the boulder. I recognized her as the fox I had seen in the clearing before. She looked up at us, calm and regal. She was watching us as we watched her.

The young foxes on the boulder were wrestling now, biting each other, playing like kittens. The bigger of the two was on top, having bowled his smaller sibling over. The smaller fox was lying on his back, biting his brother's neck, growling high-pitched growls. His brother reared away from the snapping jaws, and the smaller fox rolled him over. The two rolled across the top of the boulder and then, unexpectedly, dropped from sight as they fell off the edge of the boulder into the shadows.

Fox and I grinned at each other again.

A moment later, one of the young foxes reappeared from the shadows, jumping on top of the boulder. The other fox followed. The mother fox stood up and leapt between them, before they could start wrestling again. Moving swiftly and smoothly, she jumped down from the boulder. The young foxes followed her into the shadows.

They were gone.

"Wow," I said softly. "She has pups."

"Kits," Fox said. "That's what you call young foxes."

"That was great," I said. "She didn't seem scared of us at all. She knew we were here, but she wasn't scared."

"Of course not." Fox looked down at the clearing where the foxes had been. "I know that my mom's not an enchanted fox. I don't even think part of her became an enchanted fox. But that doesn't matter. I'm still Queen of the Foxes."

*　*　*

At the next class, Verla read a story by Tyler and one by Jose. We talked about each story for a while, and then Verla talked about heroes and villains. "Nobody is all good or all bad," she told us. "The world is painted in shades of gray."

Then she said she'd be giving us our last assignment.

When Verla said it was time for lunch, I hung back until everyone else had rushed for the door. "Do you have a question, Joan?" Verla asked.

"When my father asked me why I had to take this class, I told him I was writing a book," I said. Then I stopped, not really knowing what else to say.

"Are you writing a book?" she asked.

"I don't know. I'm writing a lot of stuff."

She nodded. "Do you want to write a book?"

I looked down at the notebook in my hands. "I don't know. I'm just a kid. I can't write a book."

"Why not?"

"I don't know how."

"I didn't know how to teach a class until I taught a class. No one ever knows how to do anything until they do it." Verla shrugged. "You invent yourself," she said. "With everything you do or say, you create who you are. You said you're writing a book—and maybe you are. I should warn you about that. You have to be careful when you make up answers. Sometimes they turn out to be true."

"So maybe I'm writing a book?" I said.

"Maybe," she said. "It may take you years to find out."

✳　✳　✳

Our last assignment was the hardest one—and the simplest one—of all. *Write a story,* Verla said. *It can be about anything you like.* We'd practice reading our stories at the next class, and then we'd do a public reading.

Our parents were invited to the last class, which would be held in a lecture hall on campus. Each of us would read our stories aloud to the group. Verla seemed to think that this was really important.

The next day, Fox and I spent hours up in the tree house, talking about stories we could write. I thought about writing another story about the wild girls—but that didn't seem quite right. That was something Fox and I had done together, and this was something I wanted to do by myself. I could write about what happens to the girl who turned into an owl—but I liked the way that story ended now. I didn't want to think about what happened next.

We talked and talked, but I still didn't know what I was writing about.

I got home later than usual. It was the night that my mom and dad went to the marriage counselor, so Mark and I usually just ate something Mom left for us. I came in through the back gate and was hurrying toward the back door when I saw Mark was sitting in a lawn chair in the backyard, drawing on his cast with a marker. He glanced up from his work and then quickly looked back at his cast.

"I wouldn't go in there if I were you," he said.

I stopped. "Yeah? Why not?"

"They're having a big fight." Mark's shoulders were hunched forward, and he kept his eyes on his cast. He was using a blue ballpoint pen to color the uniform of a masked superhero. Rather than just coloring it in solid, he was drawing lots of thin blue lines, packed close together. His cast was covered in drawings of superheroes: superheroes fighting, superheroes flying through the air, superheroes crashing through walls.

"Yeah?" I backed away from the door and sat down in another lawn chair. Mark didn't say anything else.

After a minute, I asked, "What's the fight about? Money?"

He shook his head, a tiny movement that you wouldn't notice unless you were looking for it. "Not this time."

"Then what's it's about?"

"It started because I hadn't mowed the front lawn." He looked up from his work. "Mom pointed out that my wrist was in a cast. Then Dad said, 'So whose fault is that?'"

Mom said that it was my fault all right, but it still meant I couldn't mow the lawn. And then Dad started in on Mom for wasting her time helping Mrs. Gordon. He said she was fixing up other people's yards and ignoring ours."

I thought about how happy Mom had been when we were redoing the yard for the big house on Forest Court. How could anything that made her so happy be a waste of time?

Mark was holding his pen in his hand, but he wasn't drawing. He was looking at me.

"So then what happened?" I asked.

"Mom said it wasn't a waste of time and she wasn't neglecting our yard. She kind of let him have it," Mark said. "She told him he had no right to talk to her that way. And he said he'd talk however he wanted in his own home. And she said it was her house, too."

"She was yelling back at him?"

"Not yelling, really. She wasn't loud or anything. But she wasn't letting him get away with anything. He said it was all because of that counselor, and she said it wasn't. She said he was making everyone miserable and she wasn't going to put up with it anymore. She said he was destroying this family. That was when I came out here."

It sounded really bad. "When was that?"

"About half an hour ago. I figure Mom will come out and let me know when the coast is clear."

I nodded. I sure didn't want to walk in if they were still

fighting. After a moment, Mark returned to coloring his cast.

I leaned back in the lawn chair. The air was still and warm. Mom's garden was a riot of tomatoes. The bushy plants had overgrown the wire cages that Mom had set around them at the start of the summer. They were spilling over the cages and onto the ground.

The mockingbird was sitting on the chimney, its favorite perch. As I sat and waited, it began to sing. It would sing a few notes—the call of some bird, I guessed—then it would repeat that a few times.

I thought about Mom and Dad in the house. Maybe Dad would get so mad when he heard the mockingbird that he'd stop fighting. Maybe he'd come storming out and say he was going to kill that damn bird. I didn't know if that would be a good thing or not. It would be good to stop the fight, I guess.

I was writing about the mockingbird in my notebook when Mom came out of the house. She looked really tired. Her eyes were red, as if she'd been crying. She didn't say anything at first. She just pulled up a lawn chair and sat beside us.

Then she said, "Your father won't be home for dinner."

Mark looked up from his drawing, and I closed my notebook. "I thought he was home," I said, looking at Mark.

"He was home, but he went out again."

"When's he coming back?" Mark asked.

"I don't know."

Watching my mom, I figured it wasn't a good time to ask any more questions. The three of us had dinner, and nobody really had much to say. We all went to bed early, even Mark.

Lying in bed that night, I thought about flying away. I had never thought about what it was like for the people who stayed home when someone else flew away. The house was very quiet. The light of the moon shone through my window.

I got up to go to the bathroom, and I saw that the kitchen light was on. My mom was sitting at the kitchen table. Her landscaping textbook was on the table in front of her, but she wasn't reading it. She wasn't crying. She wasn't doing anything. She was just staring into space.

"Mom?" I said quietly.

She turned to look at me. "Hey," she said softly, "what are you doing up?"

"I had to go to the bathroom." I pulled a chair up to the table and sat down across from her. "So did Dad come home?" I knew that he hadn't. I would have heard him if he had. Dad was never quiet, even when other people were sleeping.

She shook her head.

"Do you know where he went?" I asked.

"We talked about a trial separation at the marriage

counselor last week," she said. "When we were arguing, he decided to move out right away. He just packed a few things and left." She shook her head, frowning. "I was surprised. I shouldn't have been surprised, but I was."

Ask questions, Verla said. "How do you feel?" I asked her.

"Stunned, I guess. Confused. The house feels empty."

"When Dad was home, sometimes it felt too crowded," I said.

She nodded. "Sometimes it did. But now it feels empty."

Just then, the mockingbird started singing. The bird was perched on the chimney, and exuberant, glorious bursts of song echoed through the house.

"Your dad would be threatening to shoot that bird if he were here," my mom said.

I nodded.

"I've always liked that bird," my mom said.

"So have I."

I went back to my room and fell asleep listening to the mockingbird sing.

20

And Then What?

Dad didn't come home that night or the next night or the night after that. While I was at Fox's, he came home to get some stuff, and he was gone again. That's what Mark told me.

I worked on my story for the last class. I had decided to write a story that didn't have anything to do with Dad. We practiced reading our stories in class, and Verla gave us tips on how to do a better job of reading them aloud.

A week and a half after Dad moved out, the day of the final reading dawned bright and sunny. My mom drove us all to Berkeley—me and Mark and Fox and Gus.

I was surprised that Mark came to the reading. My mom had asked him if he wanted to come, and he had said he did. Since Dad had moved out, he'd been spending more time at home. He had mowed the lawn without even being asked. He and I hadn't talked about it, but I think we both wanted to help Mom as much as we could.

The lecture hall was not far from Sproul Plaza. Fox and I led the way from the parking lot. As we crossed the plaza,

I couldn't help remembering my first trip to the campus, when we had walked from BART to our first class. It had all seemed so strange then: the buildings were too big; the people, too strange and loud; the campus, too confusing. It had seemed like a land of enchantment. It still felt like an enchanted place, but now I felt right at home.

"Hey, Joan! Hey, Fox!" It was Azalea, calling to us from the Circus of Chaos table, which was set up in its usual position in the shade. "What are you up to?"

"Our class is doing a reading," I told her. I introduced her to my mom and my brother and Gus. My brother was staring at her, his eyes wide.

Azalea was looking particularly splendid that morning. Her face was painted a brilliant royal blue, the color of the sky at dusk. On her forehead and cheeks were flecks of gold, like the first stars emerging on a summer night. Her left eye was half encircled by the crescent moon.

"Would you like your face painted, in honor of the occasion?" Azalea asked my mom.

My mom blinked, a little bit startled. I looked at Azalea, and she grinned, her teeth bright white against the blue of her face. My mom glanced at her watch. "I don't know," she said. "We need to get to the lecture hall."

"We have plenty of time, Mom," I said.

"Do you think that's an appropriate way to honor the occasion?" my mom asked Azalea.

"Of course," Azalea said. "In most cultures, the painting of the face is part of any transformative ceremony."

"Is this a transformative ceremony?" my mom asked me.

Verla had told us that this presentation was important. She had talked about something called the hero's journey, where the hero went on a quest and returned to the acclaim of his community. She said this was our chance to feel the support of our community. That sounded transformative to me.

"Verla says it is," I told her.

Azalea was busy at her table, opening her box of paints, taking out her hand mirror. "So, what would you like to be?" she asked my mom.

"You mean like a clown or something like that?" my mom said.

Azalea waved a hand to encompass the world. "Think big," she said. "This morning, I woke up and decided to become the night sky. In all the universe, what would you like to be?"

"That's a big question," my mom said.

"Of course," Azalea agreed. "Those are the best kind."

My mom thought for a moment, and then said, "I'd like to be a garden."

Azalea nodded and her grin widened. "Oh, that's lovely. A garden is always in the process of becoming. Always changing. What a great thing to be." She gestured to the folding chair beside the table. "One garden, coming up. Sit down and close your eyes."

My brother and I exchanged startled looks as Mom

sat down. I hadn't really thought she'd do it. Azalea got to work.

"Be sure to put in a pumpkin," I told Azalea. "A perfect pumpkin."

My mom opened her eyes and shot me a look.

"It will be a lovely pumpkin," Azalea said.

Under her brush, my mom's face became a late-summer garden, with a crookneck squash that matched the curve of one cheek and a perfect pumpkin on the other. There were green beans, ripe tomatoes, an explosion of yellow daisies, and green leaves everywhere. When Azalea showed my mom her face in the mirror, she looked startled. "It certainly is a transformation."

"That's the name of the game," Azalea said.

"It looks great," I told my mom. Fox and Gus and Mark agreed.

"Can you paint me?" Mark asked.

Azalea painted Mark's face so that he looked like the Incredible Hulk, one of the characters that he'd had drawn on his cast. She painted Fox so that her face looked like a fox. Then she turned to me.

I shook my head, smiling. "I think I'll be myself today," I told her.

Azalea raised one eyebrow quizzically, and the moon shifted a little in the night sky. "Bold move," she said. "Good for you."

We got to the lecture hall right on time. It wasn't as large as the auditorium where Fox and I had read our story. The crowd was a lot smaller, too. Mostly people's parents.

Zoom came up with her parents and introduced them to Fox and me. They smiled a lot and seemed really happy. Zoom's dad thanked me for helping Zoom find a name she liked. They praised my mom's face paint, which I think helped her relax a little.

Al's mom came and his dad came, but they didn't talk to each other at all, and they sat on opposite sides of the auditorium. Al introduced us to both of them separately. I told his dad that I thought it was really cool that Al had a boa constrictor, and that seemed to make his dad really happy.

Bodie's parents came. His dad looked just like a professor, which he was. He wore a tweedy jacket with leather patches on the elbows. Bodie's mom wore a long dress and a flower behind her ear. She looked like someone who would play the cello in the garden every morning. She smiled when Bodie introduced us and said that she'd heard so much about us. Bodie turned red, which was funny because we'd never seen him blush.

I had asked my mom to send an invitation to my dad. She said she would send it to him, but I really didn't think he'd come. And sure enough, there was no sign of him.

All the parents milled around and talked to each other, which was kind of weird because we all figured that they were talking about us. I mean—what else did they have to talk about?

But finally, everyone sat down and we were ready to begin. Bodie read, then Ketura, then Zoom—but I couldn't tell you anything about what they had to say. I was too busy thinking about my own story.

Then it was my turn to be onstage, looking out at all the parents. "Once upon a time," I said, "there was a woman who had forgotten how to fly."

My mom was in the front row, looking very unlike herself. Through the face paint, I could see that she looked relaxed and happy. She wore the crimson glass teardrop around her neck, and I wore the matching pendant around my neck.

I wasn't wearing war paint. But that didn't matter. I didn't need the war paint. I was a different person than I had been, back then.

"She used to know how to fly," I read, "but over the years, she'd forgotten. One day, when she was cleaning out the hall closet, she found the wings she had stored there many years before. They were dusty and bedraggled, and some of the feathers had fallen off. But she took them out anyway."

That was when I saw my dad in the audience. He must have snuck in late. He was sitting in the back row, far away from everyone else. He was in the shadows, but I knew right away that the man in the back was my dad. Something about the way he propped his head up on his hand, leaning forward a little as he listened, looked familiar.

I read about how the woman's daughter had found the woman looking at her wings. Together, the mother and daughter took the wings up to the roof of the house and tried them out. The woman flew away—just as her husband came home and shouted, "Where's dinner?"

My dad sat in the shadows, listening. I don't think I'd ever seen him listening before. He was always talking, never listening. When the story was done, he clapped along with everyone else.

After everyone read their stories, coffee and cookies were served in the lobby. I was walking out of the auditorium when I saw my dad cross the lobby, heading out the door. He wasn't stopping for coffee or cookies. He wasn't going to stay and talk with the other parents. It was like he wanted to sneak away without talking to anyone.

I followed him.

I caught up with him as he was crossing Sproul Plaza. *What do you see?* Verla said. *What do you really see?*

I saw a man who looked out of place there, among the college women in bright sundresses and the young men in ragged jeans. My dad was dressed in neat slacks, a long-sleeved button-up shirt, and a sport coat. But more than that—all those college students were smiling, strolling along, and having a good time. My dad walked quickly—he was always in a hurry, impatient with anything that wasted his time. His face was set in its habitual expression: mouth in a straight line, eyes narrow. Not quite a frown, but a frown waiting to happen. He looked a little angry—but he also looked a little worried. As if he knew something was wrong, something that all these other people didn't know about. He was busy worrying and they were carefree, and it made him mad. That's what I thought, watching him just then.

"Hey, Dad!" I called. "Wait up!"

He turned to look at me, his expression changing. He didn't stop frowning, but his eyes widened a bit. He was surprised to see me. Still worried, maybe not quite so angry.

I fell into step beside him. "Thanks for coming to the reading," I said.

"I thought I'd see how you were doing in that class of yours," he said. He wasn't looking at me anymore. He was still walking across the plaza, though he had slowed his pace a tiny bit. "I didn't think you saw me."

"I saw you from the stage," I said.

"So how's that book you're writing?"

"It's all right," I said.

"Are you done yet?"

I didn't like that question. It made me feel like I was taking too long, like I was slow and should be quicker. Like maybe I was wasting time. "No," I said. "It takes a long time to write a whole book."

He didn't say anything for a minute. I was glad of that. I had halfway expected him to start lecturing me about finishing what I started or working up to my abilities or something like that. But he didn't. He asked, "Am I in your book?"

I hesitated, surprised by the question. "Yeah," I said. "Yeah, you are."

He stopped walking and turned to look at me. "I guess I'm the villain. The evil king? Is that who I am?" He was frowning then, eyebrows lowered, mouth in a grim line.

I thought about what Verla had said in class. "There aren't any heroes or villains," I said. "There are just different points of view. That's what Verla says."

He blinked, still frowning. But his frown had changed a bit—rather than just looking angry, he looked angry and a little puzzled. "Of course there are villains," he said with great confidence.

I shook my head. It felt strange, disagreeing with my dad. But I had to do it. "A villain doesn't think he's a villain," I said. "You might think he's a villain. But he thinks he's right."

"Wasn't the evil king a villain?" my dad asked. "I read that story you wrote about the wild girls. It seemed like he was a villain."

I nodded slowly. "Maybe. But I wrote that story before I took the class. I told you I had to learn more about writing. I think maybe that story is too black and white. Maybe there's room for shades of gray."

"So maybe the king wasn't so evil?"

I shrugged. "Not from his point of view."

"He yelled a lot," my dad said. He wasn't frowning anymore. He wasn't smiling, but he wasn't frowning. "Maybe he shouldn't have yelled so much. And I think maybe that king wasn't as smart as he thought he was. But maybe he wasn't evil."

"Maybe not," I said.

"I think he was just trying to keep things in order," my dad said. "Someone has to run the kingdom, after all."

I nodded, thinking that maybe I would try to write a story from the king's point of view. That would be interesting.

"Hey, Joan! How did the reading go?"

I looked toward the voice. It was Azalea, standing by the Circus of Chaos table.

My dad glanced at Azalea, frowning again. I didn't see how anyone could look at Azalea and keep frowning, but my dad managed it. I didn't think Azalea could convince Dad to get his face painted.

"The reading went fine," I told Azalea. "Dad, this is Azalea. She's with the Circus of Chaos. She taught me to walk on stilts."

"On stilts?" For a moment, my dad was too surprised to frown. "Why did you want to learn that?"

I stared at him, unable to think of an answer. Because it was fun? Because I could? I was frozen for a moment, unable to speak.

"To see the world from another point of view," Azalea said, without waiting for me to answer. "Stilt walking gives you a new outlook on life." She grinned at me. "So—do you want to get tall?"

I did. I wanted to get up on stilts even if it made my dad frown. Maybe even *because* it would make him frown.

"Sure," I said, and before my dad could say a word—

before he could tell me that walking on stilts was silly or a waste of time—I was strapping on the peg stilts. Azalea gave me a hand up, and suddenly, I was tall.

Very tall.

I looked down at my father. From above, I could see the top of his head. His hair was thinning, and his scalp was showing through. I had never noticed that before. When he looked up at me, his frown didn't seem so frightening. Or maybe he wasn't frowning as much as before. He was looking up at me, startled and amazed.

I began walking. You don't have any choice when you're on stilts. You start walking or you fall down. So I started walking, and my dad walked alongside me.

"Aren't you afraid that you'll fall?" he asked.

At that moment, I wasn't afraid of anything. "Nope." Then I took a step that was a bit too big, and I teetered a little, as if I might fall. My dad reached up to help, and I took hold of his hand. That steadied me.

He didn't say anything, but he kept holding my hand, reaching up as we walked along. I remembered when I was seven and I had learned to ride a bicycle. My dad had taken off the training wheels. He had run along beside me, holding the back of the seat to keep me from falling. When he let go, I sailed down the street, pedaling and staying up all by myself.

Now I was holding his hand as I walked on stilts. I wasn't sure whether he was helping me or I was helping him.

✷ ✷ ✷

So I guess I've written a book. I've written a bunch of pages, anyway. Some of these pages are just the way I wrote them in that notebook that Gus gave me. Some I rewrote lots of times, copying them over and over until I got them right.

After the reading, some other stuff happened. My dad didn't move back in, but he and my mom are still going to counseling. I don't know what's going to happen there.

Mom kept working with Mrs. Gordon, giving "curb appeal" to houses. It makes her happy, and she's making money doing it. So that's good.

Fox's mom is getting divorced from Gus, but that doesn't seem like a bad thing. Fox and her mom have been writing letters back and forth, and that seems to be going okay.

Fox and I have to go back to school next week. My mom asked me last night what I had learned this summer. I couldn't tell her in just a few words, so I told her I'd write about it and let her read that.

I've learned to write the truth. But to do that, I had to figure out what the truth was—and I had to realize that the truth isn't always the same for everyone. I had to realize that my truth may not be the same as your truth.

I learned about subtext and I learned to ask questions. And ask more questions. And ask even more questions. Sometimes that annoys people, but I've learned that annoying people a little bit is not always a bad thing. Asking questions is good, even if it is sometimes annoying.

I learned not to keep my head down. Oh, sure—sometimes it's a good idea, but not always. Sometimes it's a good idea to take chances, to make trouble, and to say exactly what I think.

I learned that I'm not the only loose nut around. The world is a bigger and more wonderful place than they teach us in school.

I learned to walk on stilts. I learned to hammer a nail. I learned that my mother is fond of pigs and that I have more in common with my dad than I ever knew. I learned to change my point of view.

Drop a pebble in a pond, Verla says. *Watch the ripples spread. That's what you want your writing to do.*

That's what I learned. I learned to make ripples.

So what's next?

Now that I've filled a couple of notebooks, I guess I'll get some more and I'll fill those, too. I've written one book, and I'll write another.

That, Verla says, is what writers do.

ACKNOWLEDGMENTS

Every time I finish a novel, I am struck once again by the generosity of those who have helped me along the way.

I'd like to thank the members of my writing group for reading and commenting on the novella from which this novel grew. Many thanks to Karen Fowler, Carter Scholz, Michael Blumlein, Daniel Marcus, Richard Russo, Marta Randall, Angus MacDonald, Ellen Klages, and Michael Berry.

Laurie Brandt provided thoughtful insights about Fox and Joan, the amazing Tom Sepe taught me to walk on stilts, in a class at the Crucible, and Claude Lalumière and Marty Halpern published the novella in their anthology *Witpunk*. Ellyn Hament and Zoe Kamil read and commented on the book. Their assistance was invaluable.

My husband, Dave, kept me well fed and (more or less) sane, and my agent, Jean Naggar, provided essential support and encouragement during the long process.

Finally, I gratefully acknowledge my editor, Sharyn November, whose astute editorial judgment and knowledge of her readers helped shape the book. Without her help, this would have been a very different book (and not nearly as good).

Pat Murphy's writing has won numerous awards, including the Nebula Award, the World Fantasy Award, and the Seiun Award, the latter for the best science fiction novel translated into Japanese. Her work ranges from scientifically accurate science fiction to psychological fantasy to magic realism. She also works for the Crucible (www.thecrucible.org), a nonprofit school dedicated to teaching the industrial arts and the fire arts (from blacksmithing to fire eating) and edits books for Klutz Press, a publishing enterprise that began in 1977 with *Juggling for the Complete Klutz* and today creates hands-on how-to books for kids.

For more about Pat's work, visit **www.brazenhussies. net/murphy**. For writing advice, teaching tips, and more, visit **www.verlavolante.com**.

"I met the Queen of the Foxes in 1972, when my family moved from Connecticut to California...."

Twelve-year-old Joan is sure that she is going to be miserable in her new home. Then she meets a kindred spirit: Sarah, who prefers to be called "Fox" and who lives with her writer father in a rundown house in the middle of the woods.

Joan and Sarah—Newt and Fox—spend all their spare time outside, talking and fooling around, and soon start writing stories together. When they win first place in a student fiction contest, they're recruited for a prestigious summer writing class taught by a free spirit named Verla Volante.

This is a book about friendship, the power of story, and how coming of age means finding your own answers—rather than simply taking

"A terrific mix of imagination, insight, character inventiveness and kindness create the kind of read that nourishes young minds and hearts."
—*Kirkus Reviews*

WINNER OF THE CHRISTOPHER AWARD
A *BOOK SENSE* SELECTION

ISBN 978-0-14-241245-9

9 780142 412459

50799>

EAN

speak

U.S.A $7.99 CAN. $9.00
VISIT US AT
www.penguin.com

Cover photo: Veer Images
Cover design and illustrations by
Jeanine Henderson